THE LAST DESERTER

What mystery lay behind the desertion of an Arab village by its inhabitants? And what caused the mass desertions from Dana Talani, the French Foreign Legion outpost in the Sahara? Men had unexpectedly found themselves with so much money they had lavished drinks upon their comrades — and then they were gone. The French wanted answers to these questions — questions posed to two American legionnaires, Duke and Cream . . . and in solving the desert mystery their lives came perilously close to extinction.

JOHN ROBB

THE LAST DESERTER

Complete and Unabridged

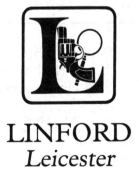

LINFORD
Leicester

First published in Great Britain

First Linford Edition
published 2011

British Library CIP Data

Robb, John.
   The last deserter. - -
   (Linford mystery library)
   1. Military deserters- -Fiction. 2. France.
   Armee. Legion etrangere- -Fiction.
   3. Millionaires- -United States- -Fiction.
   4. Suspense fiction. 5. Large type books.
   I. Title II. Series
   823.9'14–dc22

   ISBN 978–1–4448–0693–9

Published by
F. A. Thorpe (Publishing)
Anstey, Leicestershire

Set by Words & Graphics Ltd.
Anstey, Leicestershire
Printed and bound in Great Britain by
T. J. International Ltd., Padstow, Cornwall

This book is printed on acid-free paper

1

The village

Halusa was an Arab village — once. Now only the bleak and lifeless bones of the place were left. The mud hovels remained. And the narrow, filth-filled alleys. The market place, too, was still there. But the people were gone. The men and the women, the old and the young, the strong and the weak — all had disappeared.

Now, in its weird quiet, Halusa was as though in some fantastic moment all of mankind had been swept from the earth. It was the undisputed domain of the insects, the vultures, and the wild dogs. They moved through the place at will, but there was little there to satiate their primitive appetites. They had quickly consumed what had been left by the inhabitants.

By day the village baked silently under the Sahara sun. By night it was swept by chill breezes. And as the days and the nights followed on each other, even the bones of Halusa seemed to decay.

Sand formed deep over the hard mud paths. It spread, too, on the hovels so that the walls began to crack under the weight. And the crude wood structures in the market place were being eaten into and weakened by the invading beetles.

Perhaps, if it had been left thus for a few months instead of only a few weeks, Halusa would have passed from the sight of man, and travellers would have searched for it in vain. But it was found in time. It was found before the sand could bury and conceal it.

The mystery of Halusa was discovered by eleven Zara Arabs who were escorting their caravan of sixteen camels from the foot of the Atlas mountains to the trading centre and Legion outpost at Dana Talani.

The animals were loaded with silks, spices, coffee, and other merchandise, which would find a ready sale in Dana Talani. They had been moving for three days. Days in which the camels had snorted protests at their burdens and at the vicious whip cuts that drove them on.

It was only because one of the water bags had developed a leak that the caravan had turned slightly off the usual trading course and towards Halusa. After a long discussion the Zaras had decided that it would be safer to avail themselves of the water hole which existed there.

It was during the early morning hours that they entered Halusa. The sun was only just up and it had not yet gained any of its violent heat.

At first the Zaras thought that the people of Halusa were still sleeping. They even found energy to make crude jokes on the subject of their supposed laziness and they laughed as they led the camels down the single main street.

But soon the laughter died away.

At first it was replaced by dazed silence, then by exclamations of wonder and fear. They peeped fearfully into the hovels. As they found each one deserted of human life or even human remains, their fear grew in proportion.

After a few minutes one old Zara threw

his arms heavenwards and went down on his knees.

'The place is accursed,' he called. 'This is a blight from Allah!'

Then he rose again and ran stumbling towards his camels. The others followed, wailing and mouthing their terror. And as they rode out of the village, the howls of the wild dogs joined with the expressions of human woe.

It was four days later that the strange story of Halusa was being told and discussed at Dana Talani.

For once, the Zara traders forgot about their merchandise. They were too busy answering the incredulous questions and unconsciously stimulating the wild flow of rumour that swept the town within an hour of their arrival.

It was not long before the tale reached the ears of Major Pylo, the officer commanding the garrison there. The facts, such as were known, were supplied to him by Captain D'Avalon.

D'Avalon said: 'Of course, we must allow for exaggeration. But none the less, the basic facts must certainly be true, and it seems strange, does it not, that the entire population of a village should disappear?'

Major Pylo grunted. He pulled at his pipe and blinked into the flames like a mystic searching for enlightenment. Then he opened a drawer in his desk and pulled out a sheaf of typewritten papers. Each folio was marked 'Confidential,' but, in fact, there was little that need be secret on those sheets. They merely listed all the towns and villages of French Morocco, with their populations and trading activities.

Pylo moved his finger down until he found the name he wanted.

'Between three and four hundred inhabitants at Halusa,' he said. 'It's a minor oasis. They seem to exist by growing maize and breeding goats.'

Captain D'Avalon allowed a flicker of exasperation to cross his features. He and Pylo were old friends. They respected each other. But in temperament they were very unalike. That was why the quick, darting mind of D'Avalon was sometimes annoyed by the slower, apparently more pedestrian approach of his senior.

'I know Halusa quite well,' D'Avalon said crisply. 'I've been there quite often in the course of patrols, but not recently.'

Pylo puffed smoke and smoothed down his white hair with a thin hand.

'Then no doubt you will want to go out there to look into this business, although I feel there is some quite reasonable and logical explanation for it all.'

D'Avalon smiled and lit a cigarette. He crossed to the map that was suspended on the wall of Pylo's room.

'*Oui*, I suppose that is true — but I can't imagine what the explanation can be. Look at the position of Halusa. It is well off the normal trade routes and nearly fifty miles from the next village. That means that the people who leave Halusa must travel a long way before they can get new supplies. Even so, there'd be nothing unusual in the *men* departing — particularly the young men. They might find many reasons for doing so. But this is not just a matter of the men. They have all gone, including the women and children . . . '

Pylo interrupted with a word of caution.

'That's according to what the caravan traders say. It need not be correct.'

'I think it will be correct. Such people may well go wrong on matters of detail. But this is no detail. It is the main fact of their whole report — that the village was entirely abandoned. It is not likely to be a mass invention, and all those Zaras are certain about it.'

Pylo glanced at the map.

'*Trés bien* . . . it will be quite a long patrol out to Halusa. You'll be away for more than a week. How many men do you want to take?'

D'Avalon was the kind of officer who was seldom in doubt. He nearly always made his decisions long before the need for them arose. Therefore he answered promptly.

'Ten men from my company.'

Pylo glanced up from his desk. He seemed slightly surprised.

'Only ten! Surely it is rather a small force for such a long march.'

'I don't think so. Remember, this is an

investigation, and the fewer men the better. Those I take will be carefully chosen for intelligence.'

Pylo smiled wryly. He was under no illusion as to the mental qualities of the men in the Foreign Legion.

'You will find yourself facing a hard task. Ten clever legionnaires will indeed be difficult to find!'

D'Avalon smiled too.

'Nonetheless, I think they can be produced. The Legion is the refuge of many strange characters and they all have one thing in common — great personal misfortune. But not all are fools. I will find my ten and between us we will discover what happened in the village of Halusa.'

2

The Deserters

The garrison at Dana Talani had been paid that morning. Not much, of course. It never is much in the Legion. But it was enough for those who were off duty to sit in the wine shops and cafés from sundown until a few minutes before the time for midnight *appel*.

Just a few hours. A few fast, unimportant hours that would pass unnoticed in the lives of most people. But to the legionnaires they were islands of escape.

During that time they drank. And as they drank the fumes from the cheap and vinegary wine rose in fuddled clouds into their heads. Then their senses became dulled. Their memories, too. And that was good, for few of them wished to remember.

Under such conditions they could quarrel, boast, shout and threaten and no one would stop them. Temporarily the chains of Legion discipline were gone. They were free men again. Like other men. They were people with wills of their own. No longer were they military mercenaries.

Duke Connor was at one of the wine shops. At El Tula's. As always, he was with Cream.

Both Duke and Cream were among the few exceptions that night. Neither of them was drunk.

But on the other hand, neither was exactly sober.

In fact, those two Americans, one white and the other coloured, were in a pleasant state of alcoholic mellowness. The state in which a man has complete control of his senses without being unduly bothered by them. In other words, the condition of quiet mastery and self-confidence. The condition in which one is wise and brilliant, tolerant and understanding . . . in one's own opinion.

They were sitting in a quiet comer. Anyway, in a comparatively quiet corner. It was impossible to entirely escape the row in that place. At some tables legionnaires were singing. And even when the songsters agreed on the words they differed about the tune. On a small and unsafe looking platform a pretty Arab girl was dancing. She was encouraged by a pair of turbaned musicians who forced peculiar noises out of long tubes.

Both Duke and Cream had their tunics unfastened as they sprawled opposite each other over the small wicker table.

Cream rubbed the jet blackness of his huge chest. At one time, not so long ago, Cream had been one of America's best heavyweight ring prospects. That prospect had now vanished, but he still had all the physical equipment.

Cream said: 'Maybe this ain't the same at Broadway, but ah sure think it makes a nice sorta change.'

Duke grinned. His slim, wiry frame made a contrast with that of his black friend.

In their partnership, it was Cream who provided the physical strength and Duke the mental equipment. But that didn't mean that Cream was a fool. He wasn't.

And Duke wasn't any weakling either.

'Any place'd seem good after sweating it out in barracks for a couple of weeks without dough to go any place,' Duke said. 'Right now, El Tula's wine shop's got everything Broadway can offer. It's kinda funny though . . . when we're out in the desert we dream about getting back to Dana Talani. We think it'd be good just to sit in the barracks at night and be chased around the parade ground in the day. But after a couple of days of it, we start to think that maybe it wasn't so bad in the desert. I figure that in the Legion no one's ever pleased for long, and that's because no one's got much to be pleased about.'

Cream rolled himself a cigarette. He drew the acrid tobacco deep into his lungs, as he watched the Arab girl's sinuous dancing. Then he took a long pull of *vin ordinaire.*

He asked: 'Have you thought about this story that's goin' around about Halusa?'

Duke nodded. He looked puzzled.

'I guess everybody's thought about it since those traders came in with the

12

report. They wouldn't phoney up a yarn like that. It looks to me like it's gonna be one of the mysteries of the desert. Some durned strange things do happen in the Sahara. Things no one can explain, I figure this could be one of them.'

Cream was going to say something. But his voice was drowned by a sudden burst of laughter from a nearby table. Seven legionnaires were sitting there and they were more drunk than most of the other customers. Each had his own bottle of wine in front of him. A richly robed Arab was with them.

Duke glanced towards them. Then he said to Cream:

'Those boys sure are having a brisk time.'

'Yeah. And they are always together these days,' Cream said. 'And they could go out at nights when the rest of the garrison was broke. Ah guess they musta cleaned up at cards.'

Duke said he thought so too. But he idly wondered where they played the pasteboards to be able to sling around the dough they were using. Although those seven legionnaires were in his own company, Duke did not know any of them well. He knew their names, of course, and at odd times, had spoken to all of them. But that was all.

He was still thinking about them when one of the seven got up. That was Legionnaire Goetler. Goetler was a big-boned Pole. Once he'd been a miner. He swayed slightly as he moved towards the exit. On the way he noticed Duke and Cream. He changed course and turned towards them, ending by leaning heavily on their table so that the fragile structure creaked.

'You will have a bottle with me — eh?' he asked in the debased French that is common to all races of legionnaires.

Duke glanced at Cream. They both hesitated. They had the natural doubt about accepting a favour from a drunken man. Goetler seemed to sense that hesitation. He said:

'You fear for my pocket, eh? You don't need to. Me — I've plenty of money and this may be my last chance to buy you a little drink.'

At the last sentence Duke and Cream looked up sharply at him. But Goetler had already forgotten what he'd said. He was ordering two bottles of wine from an Arab waiter.

By now his friends had followed Goetler. They were waiting by the door, obviously impatient for him to leave with them. Goetler saw them, waved loosely at Duke and Cream, then led the way out. Their Arab companion had already gone.

El Tula's was much quieter with their absence.

The new wine arrived. On the platform the Arab girl and her two musicians went on with their performance. Duke regarded his bottle for quite a time before he opened it. He was still thinking as he drank. Eventually he said:

'I wonder what Goetler meant about this being his last chance to buy us a drink.'

'He was drunk,' Cream said flatly, as though that explained everything.

'I know. But no guy says that sorta thing unless he's gotten something at the back of his mind . . . but maybe I'm stupid to spend tonight thinking about Goetler and his buddies. Come on — let's drink . . . '

The bottles were empty at ten minutes to midnight. Both Duke and Cream considered they'd timed their drinking nicely. There was just time to get back into barracks before *appel.*

That extra wine had made a difference. They sang as they made their way through the alleys of Dana Talani. They even sang as they passed through the main barrack gates until the shrieking voice of the sergeant of the guard shook them into a reluctant silence.

B Company barrack room was exactly like all the others. It held one hundred and twenty men. The rows of hard bunks were drawn up along each side of the room in two rows of sixty. There was a crude wood table in the middle where the legionnaires could write letters — if they wished to write letters, which was seldom. There was no glass in the windows. But they were barred, like those of a prison. The walls were of crude grey stone. Behind some of the bunks the wall was decorated with photographs — mostly photographs of women or some half-forgotten scene of home.

Sergeant Collat strutted in to take *appel*.

That was the most noticeable fact about Sergeant Collat — he strutted. He was a small Frenchman with quick, bird-like movements. His face, too, had something in common with a bird. It was thin, and the large nose was not unlike a beak. On the rare occasions when Collat had been seen without his hat on, it was noted that his dark head was shaped on much the same lines as that of an eagle. It was narrow, yet it was powerful.

Collat held before him the list of names of those in B Company, although he almost knew them by heart.

Midnight *appel* was one of three daily roll calls. But it had a difference from the two others. At this one the legionnaires were not required to parade. They did not even have to be dressed. A man could answer his name while lying on his bunk if he wished. And that was how many of them answered now. But Duke and

Cream were sitting on their bunks and talking when Collat came in. They remained sitting while he went through the roll.

For the first minute all went according to the orthodox ritual. First Collat barked the name. A legionnaire called back '*Oui, mon sergent.*' Then Collat would pencil a tick on his list.

The first hitch came when the name of Legionnaire Hass was called. Hass was a Dutchman. Hass was also a moderately reliable soldier. True, three years before he'd murdered a storekeeper in Amsterdam. But that was no concern of the Legion. And it certainly did not worry Sergeant Collat. What did worry Collat was the fact that Hass did not answer to his name.

Collat repeated it, his voice rising to a shriek.

'*Legionnaire Hass . . . repondez.*' Still no answer.

A quiver of interest seemed to run through the barrack room. To be late for *appel* was a serious offence. Any offence was serious in the Legion. For this one,

18

Hass would receive at least fifteen days' pack drill plus loss of pay.

Collat dropped his voice a few octaves and said: 'Has anyone seen Hass?'

Several legionnaires spoke at the game time. Yes, it seemed they had seen Hass at El Tula's. Drunk? Well — perhaps a little.

Collat said something under his breath. Something that would not have reassured Hass had he heard it. Then he continued with *appel.*

But not for long.

A few seconds later it was found that Legionnaire Goetler was missing. In answer to questions Sergeant Collat established that he'd been drinking with Hass. There was a vicious shadow over the N.C.O.'s face as he proceeded. By the time he'd finished he'd marked a total of seven absentees. It was without precedent. A search party would have to go out to find them immediately.

Collat was not considered a bad N.C.O. so far as Legion N.C.O.s went. There were others whose brutality was far more developed. But nonetheless, Collat did not waste any sympathy on erring

19

legionnaires. He almost licked his lips in anticipation of the punishments to come as he left the barrack room and strutted towards the company office.

Immediately the door closed behind him every man in the company started to talk. They talked across the heavy blackness, for the oil lamps had been extinguished.

It was Duke who made the point that brought about a sudden silence in the barrack room. Although quietly spoken, his words cut across the general hubbub.

'Maybe you haven't noticed,' he said, 'but all those boys who are missing tonight were drinking together at El Tula's. And they had plenty of dough. And they went out of the place early with an Arab. Come to think of it, those seven guys seemed mighty friendly with that Arab. And Goetler did say he wouldn't have a chance to buy me another drink. That sounds like he was preparing to desert . . . with six others . . . '

3

The Europeans

Major Pylo's grey hair was slightly disarrayed as he looked upon the rigid figure of Sergeant Collat. He rubbed his hand through it again and it became yet more untidy.

Then he asked: 'You are sure there's absolutely no trace of these men?'

In spite of his position at attention, Collat permitted himself a slight nod of the head.

'That is so, *mon officier.* They might have dissolved into the air. There is no trace of them. No one mentions seeing them after they left the café with an Arab. Almost every building in the town has been searched. Mounted men have swept the area outside, checking all the possible escape routes. The result is always the same — zero.'

Pylo played with his pencil. He rolled it

across his desk and his brow was furrowed.

Eventually he said: 'I don't think we need search any further. Deserters never escape for long. Sooner or later they will be brought back — or they'll die in the desert. Perhaps it is best that the desert claims their lives, for if it does not the Legion surely shall.'

Sergeant Collat saluted, took a pace back, turned, then went out.

After he'd gone Captain D'Avalon, who had been standing unobtrusively in a corner, came up to the desk. He was sucking the tip of his cane — a habit of D'Avalon's when he was in a thoughtful mood.

He said: 'Disappearances seem to be becoming too fashionable. First an entire Arab village. Now a party of seven legionnaires.'

Pylo pulled out his pipe. He stuffed dark and strong tobacco into the bowl.

'*Oui* . . . that was also going through my mind. It seems impossible that it can be anything but coincidence, but it is very extraordinary. Still . . . the deserters are a small matter, which will ultimately be settled. It is this village of Halusa that is our main trouble. The general staff will want a full report. Try to get all the information you can on what possessed these people to quit the place. I feel . . . '

The door opened. An orderly came in and saluted.

He said that Zamo wished to speak with the major urgently.

Pylo did not hesitate.

'Send him in,' he said.

While they were waiting Pylo and D'Avalon glanced at each other. It was almost a knowing glance. Zamo was an important man to the garrison commander at Dana Talani. He was a silk trader, making frequent caravan trips to and from the Atlas Mountains. He was also reputed to be a man of some wealth. But that alone was not what made him so valuable. Zamo was also an intelligence agent for the Legion command. For years he had made reports on what he had seen and heard during his trips across the desert.

Mostly the information was of little value, but sometimes he had produced a fragment of fact that had proved vital. Unlike many other Arab agents, he was known to be completely reliable, always accurate. And he would not ask for an interview urgently unless he had information of great importance. Usually Zamo's messages were written out by him and reached Pylo with all other intelligence reports.

Zamo did not make an impressive entrance. He was one of those men who had grown so fat he seemed to have become out of balance.

He almost tripped over his robes as he advanced towards the desk and he almost tore them as he slumped his round little shape onto a chair that D'Avalon had placed ready. There was a beaming smile on Zamo's fleshy brown face. But that did not mean anything. Zamo was always smiling. He got a lot out of life and he was well satisfied with it.

Pylo gave him a cigarette and lighted it for him. It was not often that Zamo came into the garrison commander's office, and when he did Pylo saw he was made welcome.

'You have urgent information for me?'

Zamo nodded and the smile deepened, as though in some way he found the fact vastly amusing.

'Yes, your humble servant thinks it is urgent.'

He had a weak, squeaky voice, which he reinforced with many gestures. He went on: 'I have just arrived with my caravan and so have only just been told of the mystery of Halusa. But Halusa is not the only village which is deserted . . . '

Pylo jerked forward, his heavy eyebrows suddenly raised. D'Avalon bent his cane between his hands.

'Not the only village!' Pylo repeated subconsciously. 'You mean you have heard of others?'

'I have seen others. Two of them. This time I took the long route back and found just such utter desolation at Valan and Tuku as I've heard told of Halusa. In these two villages there was not a person there. Nothing. Only the animals and insects.'

Pylo breathed heavily and audibly. His pipe had gone out but he did not bother to relight it. He asked: 'Do you know why these people have left?'

Zamo raised his podgy hands to express ignorance.

'No one knows why. But some say it is an evil spirit which has . . . '

'Yes . . . I'm sure there are plenty who are saying that,' Pylo cut in. 'But such explanations won't satisfy the general staff at Algiers. Have you any other information which might help?'

Zamo nodded emphatically.

'Indeed, yes. But I have not seen this with mine own eyes. It comes to me through the vision of others. They say that hundreds of Arabs have been moving west across the desert. Whole families, including the smallest children. They have been carried on camels and mules.'

Major Pylo had almost exhausted his capacity for astonishment. His face was expressionless as he regarded Zamo.

'Whole families . . . are you satisfied that this information is accurate?'

For a second the smile faded from Zamo's face. He did not like any reflection on the reliability of his reports.

He was proud of their accuracy. Apprecia-
tive, too, of the liberal secret payments
which they earned for him,

'I am quite satisfied or I would not
have spoken thus to you.'

D'Avalon bent his stick so far that it
threatened to snap. He asked: 'Did they
seem to be moving voluntarily and to one
especial area?'

'It is difficult to say, *capitaine*. I am
told they were accompanied by armed
white men . . . '

'Armed white men!'

Both Pylo and D'Avalon repeated the
words together.

'Yes, it is so. White men with modern
weapons in their hands. They were
mounted on horses and seemed to be
leading rather than driving my people
towards the Atlas Mountains.'

They questioned Zamo for several
minutes. But he'd already told them as
much as he knew. He left after receiving
Pylo's thanks.

After a long interval Pylo said: '*Mon
Dieu* . . . just what is happening?'

D'Avalon sat in the chair vacated by

the Arab. He spoke more slowly than usual, as though weighing the implication of his words.

'This is not the first time that this has happened. Thirty years ago the Bormone Arabs evacuated a large number of villagers before starting their long war against the Legion. They did that because they believed the Legion might seize their families and hold them as hostages.'

Pylo said he remembered.

'I was a cadet at St. Cyr at the time,' he muttered.

D'Avalon added: 'Yet . . . somehow I do not think war is the reason today. For one thing, the Arabs now know we do not take hostages. For another, the desert is quiet. We've had no trouble for months and at this very moment all the most powerful Arab leaders are in Paris wrangling over a new treaty.'

Pylo remembered his pipe was out. He relit it. Then he said: 'Your last point is conclusive. The Arabs could never go to war while their leaders were in Paris. No . . . the reason of thirty years ago is no longer the reason of today.'

D'Avalon uncoiled his taut figure from the chair and moved towards the wall map. On his way he picked up a pencil from the desk. With the pencil he drew circles round three marked places — Halusa, Valan, Taku. He joined the circles with straight lines. Then he turned to the major.

'Do you notice anything about that?' he asked.

From his chair Pylo studied the map.

'*Oui* . . . all three villages are within easy reach of the Atlas Mountains. In fact, they seem to be the nearest small villages to the mountains. And they are closely grouped together.'

'That is so . . . and Zamo said the people were trekking in the direction of the mountains. It is in the mountains that we'll find the reason and in a locality directly opposite these villages, I think.'

Pylo smiled. It was a slightly weary smile. He was used to the impetuosity of his junior. In fact, he liked him for it. But he never allowed D'Avalon to rush him whither he did not want to go.

'That may well be so. But I do not intend to do anything just yet.'

D'Avalon looked incredulous.

'Don't intend to do anything! But surely it is vital that we act immediately!'

'Action itself does not necessarily achieve useful results, *mon ami*. One has to be certain that the action is sensible. Quite obviously, you want to take these ten men of yours into the desert. You want to examine the villages first, then go on to the Atlas Mountains. But I do not think that by so doing you will achieve anything . . . *non,* I propose to wait a few days before giving you your head. I have an idea that in that time we may learn something useful here in Dana Talani.'

4

El Tula's Wine Shop

The last parade of the day was over. For nearly twelve hours, since six in the morning they had sweated on the parade square. During the morning they had been taken in arms drill. The familiar motions of throwing a Lebel rifle around were repeated until they were more familiar still.

Then they went on the outdoor range. They fired at targets at ranges from seventy to three hundred yards. Precision fire, rapid fire, controlled fire — they'd done it all.

Then bayonet practice against straw-filled dummies with Sergeant Collat yelling deprecations . . .

It had been a typical day of 'refresher' training. A training that was designed to make them yet more efficient fighting machines when they next went into the desert.

Now it was over. Except for the unfortunate ones who were on guard duty, the garrison was free until midnight.

For the first hour after being dismissed the men of B Company did the only thing possible — they did nothing at all. They lay sprawled on their bunks in the barrack room, breathing hard, their eyes closed, waiting for energy to flow back into their exhausted limbs.

Then gradually they started to talk.

A thin-faced Cockney named Biggin was the first. Biggin was always the first to talk and the last to stop. He was the sort of prattling, cheerful man who'd have died in agony if he'd ever lost his voice.

Biggin started to tell the man in the next bunk a long and disordered story about how he'd been invited to eat a free meal in an expensive restaurant at Algiers by a visiting tourist. It appeared that, due to an incredible chain of circumstances, Biggin not only failed to get the meal free, but was flung into jail for refusing to pay the bill.

The story went on and on. But the man in the next bunk to Biggin wasn't listening. Legionnaire Iila never did listen to Biggin. There was a good reason for that. Iila was a Belgian and he didn't understand a word of English — particularly Cockney English. But that was something that Biggin didn't know.

Not that it was likely to have worried him if he had known. Biggin only asked silence of his audience. He didn't bother about attention.

' . . . I make a grab at 'is froat and I says to 'im I says . . . '

His story jangled on.

But it served one purpose. It gradually woke up the others. One by one they started talking until Biggin's voice was only one of many. They talked in many languages, but the debased pidgin French dominated, for they all understood that — except perhaps Legionnaire Biggin.

Duke rolled a couple of cigarettes. He passed one over the intervening space to Cream's bunk. He said slowly: 'I've been thinking a lot today about those desertions and I'm gonna admit I'm mighty curious. Not that I blame those boys for trying to get away. I don't. If they think they can get away from this man's army then I wish them luck. But I'd still like to know the pitch.'

Cream yawned and stretched his huge frame.

He said he felt the same way.

Duke added: 'So I figure maybe we'll go back to El Tula's wine shop tonight. I've a hunch those boys were helped and the help came from inside that joint.'

Cream turned his head towards Duke and bared his white teeth.

'Is you thinkin' of desertin' too. Duke?'

Duke laughed.

'No. I contracted to serve five years and I figure on seeing it through. But I'd sure like to know how Goetler's boys got away.'

For the second night running they went to El Tula's.

It was early when they arrived and the place was less than half full. They took the same table as on the previous occasion. And because of the wine that had been bought for them then, they now had enough francs left to buy themselves another bottle.

They had been in about half an hour

and the place was starting to fill when the Arab came in. The same Arab who had been with the seven deserters.

For one of his race, he was a powerfully built man. He carried himself with the solid certainty of one who is confident of his own strength. His robes were of heavily brocaded white silk and the turban flowed down to below his shoulders. A jewelled knife was inserted through a purple sash that stretched round his middle.

He sat at the table next to Duke and Cream. A servant came scurrying towards him and gave a quick salaam. Obviously he was regarded as a customer of importance. The Arab hesitated, as though carefully considering what to drink, then he ordered a bottle of amontillado. This Portuguese wine was only drunk by the wealthy in Dana Talani.

When it arrived he sipped it with the care of a connoisseur. While trying not to appear obvious about it, Duke watched him carefully.

Suddenly the Arab raised his head and Duke had no time to turn away. Their eyes met.

The Arab smiled. He had harsh and prominent features. That smile did little to relieve them. It played on his thin brown lips, but not on his eyes.

He spoke to Duke in French. It was good, educated French.

'*Mes legionnaires,* will you not join me? I am very alone at this table.'

The invitation was put pleasantly enough. On a hunch, Duke decided to accept. This looked like being the lead he was looking for. As they got up a big grin spread over Cream's ebony face. 'Maybe we're gonna have some more free drink,' he whispered. 'Ah figure we're doin' damned well.'

Cream was less interested than Duke in the background to the desertions. But he was very interested in the prospect of a night's hospitality. He was human.

As they sat at his table the Arab bowed to them. This time he spoke in English. Fluent English.

'I gather you are Americans,' he said evenly. 'Permit me to introduce myself. I am Rakal and I'm a merchant from Algiers.'

'Yeah, we thought you weren't from around these parts,' Duke said. 'We hadn't noticed you until yesterday.'

'I've been here only a few days and I fear I must depart soon . . . but what will you drink?'

Duke indicated their bottle of cheap wine. Rakal was not impressed. He shrugged his shoulders in a deprecating way.

'Pray have something a little more palatable — another *amontillado*, yes?'

A further bottle was ordered. The place became busier and the Arab girl started to sing on the stage. Rakal talked with them. He talked well about many things. It became evident that he'd quickly assessed Duke as being far above the normal mental level of a legionnaire and he treated him accordingly.

He spoke of trading conditions in the east, of the French government's plans for irrigation and industrial development in Morocco. Though Duke had decided from the start that he did not like Rakal, he was bound to admit that his conversation was interesting. He was a man of knowledge and authority.

Then he mentioned that only a few months before he had been on a business visit to New York. Both Duke and Cream looked up quickly at this.

Cream said: 'So you've just been in New York, mistah? Say, ah sure do wish ah'd been with you. Me and Duke both come from there. I'm from Harlem . . . '

It was spoken from the heart. Rakal smiled at Cream. It was almost a gentle smile.

'Do you wish to go back?'

The question was inserted casually. Cream's big dark eyes were dreamy as he answered.

'Ah'll say I do. But it won't be for a couple of years yet. And that goes for Duke, too. We have to wait that time mister, for our service to be up.'

Rakal sipped his wine. Then he offered them cigarettes. They were carried in a platinum case of western design.

He asked: 'What will you do when you get back to New York — if you get back?'

For a moment Duke felt a surge of annoyance. He knew what Rakal was getting at. On discharge the Legion didn't provide its ex-soldiers with the means of getting back to their homes. They were only given travel papers back to the place where they had enlisted. It was one of the many rough aspects of Legion service. But Duke didn't like to be reminded of it by this Arab.

'We'll get back okay some way,' Duke told him. 'We'll have to work our passage, I guess.'

Rakal did not reply immediately. He looked carefully at Duke under heavy, half closed eyelids.

Then he said: 'I do not wish to seem impertinent. But I know that every legionnaire has a secret reason for enlisting and always it is some — er — some misfortune. Therefore I presume neither of you is exactly . . . well, exactly fond of being in that army . . . '

Again the words were offered casually, with just a trace of sympathy. Duke sensed a bait. He decided to bite. Both he and Cream had enlisted after running out on a South American coffin ship that had put in at Algiers. A ship that they were certain was scheduled to sink at sea so that the owners could claim insurance. That was why they'd quitted the crew. But he decided to give out the idea that maybe their reason was more serious than that.

'We enlisted because the cops were wanting us,' he said with perfect truth, since all ship deserters were wanted by the police but not often hunted with any great enthusiasm. 'And you're right about not being fond of this lousy outfit. We're not.'

Rakal smiled. It was a triumphant smile.

'That was what I thought. It is well known that France treats her foreign soldiers badly — even brutally.'

Duke nodded. 'It ain't any feather bed outfit.'

Rakal ordered more wine. Deliberately he turned the conversation to other matters until it was served. Then he returned to the subject.

'Then you'd be interested in getting out of the Legion before your time has expired?'

Duke gazed at him with bland innocence.

He felt a flicker of excitement and he was also enjoying this conversation. It was sheer curiosity that had brought him to El Tula's and it seemed it could not have been better rewarded.

'Sure we would. Do you know seven guys deserted last night? They musta felt the same way as us. But we ain't aiming to desert. That's a mug's game. They hardly ever get away. You need dough and organisation to get out of this army and legionnaires don't have either.'

The last bit was thrown in on another of Duke's hunches

Again the hunch paid off.

'Both could be provided.'

There were a few moments of silence while they absorbed the information. A silence that was broken when a blind beggar who had slipped into the wine shop was ejected by noisy and irate waiters.

When the commotion subsided Duke said: 'You mean you could help us to desert?'

Although all the time he had been speaking quietly, Rakal lowered his voice still further.

'Yes ... I think I could, although something would be required of you in return.'

'What? We haven't got dough. You know that.'

He shook his head.

'Not money my friends. A little — er — service, perhaps.'

In the last minute Duke's curiosity had mounted tenfold. This looked like being something much bigger than he'd suspected. He asked what sort of service.

'A little work, perhaps. But pleasant work suitable for men of your intelligence. And at the end of it you would be comparatively rich men when you left for America.'

Duke drained his glass and refilled it.

'I'd like to know more,' he told Rakal. 'I guess you've got us both interested.'

Rakal raised a hand that was thickly clustered with rings.

'Then you must trust me as I am trusting you. I am relying on your sensible desire to leave the Legion. For the moment I can't tell you more.'

Duke said: 'But you just can't leave it

like this . . . you've given us hope. We wanta know what you want us to do.'

Again Rakal gave them cigarettes before speaking.

'Would you be prepared to leave tomorrow?'

The casualness was gone. He spoke with brisk authority. It almost took Duke by surprise.

'Sure we would — if the proposition was right. What do we do?'

'You return here tomorrow night and wait for me . . . but there are only two of you. At least three are needed to make it worthwhile. Do you know of a comrade who is trustworthy and feels the same as you?'

Duke didn't hesitate.

'I know of a lot.'

'Then bring at least one of them with you. But be sure none of you talk. Silence is to your advantage as well as ours. When you hear of what I have to offer tomorrow you'll be glad you met me . . . meantime, here is some money so you will not be embarrassed while you await me.'

He passed some franc notes to Duke.

43

They were offered and taken so quickly that no one noticed.

Then Rakal rose, bowed, and was gone from the wine shop.

And for a long time afterwards Duke and Cream looked at the door through which he had passed.

It was Cream who said: 'You ain't serious, are you?'

At first Duke did not seem to hear him. Then he turned towards Cream with a start.

'In a way I was serious. It was just a plain, honest American wish to know what goes on that brought me into this joint. I wanted to know just how Goetler and his boys had organised their desertion and I was ready to wish them a whole lot of luck. But now I'm not so sure I feel that way. That guy Rakal ain't healthy. In fact, he's almighty bad. And something tells me he's pitching a game that can mean a whole lot of trouble for a lot of people.

'Mass desertions from the Legion aren't organised out of charity. And I've just been thinking of those other mass desertions. The ones from the Arab villages. Maybe my imagination's going wild, but I'm wondering if there could be a tie-up.'

Cream said: 'Ah just can't see how there can be a tie-up. Those two things are not the same.'

Duke gave him a slow grin. But there wasn't much humour in it. In fact. his face was set in lines of hard decision.

'I've a hunch they could be the same,' he said. 'And right now my hunches are paying off. We're going back to barracks. And when we get there we're gonna make a report to Captain D'Avalon.'

Major Pylo and Captain D'Avalon listened carefully to Duke and Cream. It was Duke who did most of the talking. They interrupted only occasionally when a point was not clear.

When they had finished Pylo leaned heavily forward on his desk.

He said: 'Mes legionnaires, you were right in coming to me. By so doing you have further improved your already excellent service records. I will wish to discuss your information with Captain

D'Avalon. Wait outside. You will be wanted again.'

When Duke and Cream had saluted and marched out, Pylo turned to D'Avalon.

He said: '*Ma foi*! This is becoming a nightmare. What is happening in Morocco?'

D'Avalon rubbed the thick dark bristles on his chin He had been called from his bed for the interview.

'It is more important to decide what we're going to do,' he suggested.

'We could arrest this Arab when he appears at the wine shop tomorrow. There are ways of making him talk.'

D'Avalon was not impressed.

'That would achieve little. I think there is only one means of handling this situation.'

'*Oui*? I think I know what you're going to say, but do not let me stop you from saying it.'

'Those two legionnaires had better go to the wine shop tomorrow as arranged and take another man with them. They must conduct themselves as though still wanting to desert. Then, when they know as much as possible, they must report back to us.'

'Report back! They may not be able to do so — not if they are to be smuggled away that very night as apparently the seven others were.'

D'Avalon said firmly: 'That is the sort of chance which must be faced. We do not run the risk, of course. It is the legionnaires who will be doing that if they agree. We can't order them to undertake such work. But I know these two men. I am confident they will be glad to say yes and find some means of getting the facts to us.'

Pylo smoked a few puffs from his pipe. Then he put it down. It did not taste as pleasant as usual. He said:

'They may well lose their lives and for their own safety must not discuss the matter with their comrades . . . '

He paused as though a sudden thought had struck him. Then he added with a smile: 'I was right when I said I thought we'd learn something useful here in Dana Talani . . . '

5

Into the Desert

The choice of the man who was to go with them was left to Duke and Cream. They chose an Englishman. They chose the garrulous Legionnaire Biggin.

There were good reasons for this. One was that with Biggin there was not much language difficulty, although he occasionally produced a Cockney phrase that was beyond Duke and Cream. And although the most active part of Biggin's head was his tongue, he still knew when to keep quiet and he had plenty of common sense.

In fact, like most Cockneys, Biggin possessed a highly nimble mind. He had nerve, too. His desert fighting record showed that.

The situation was presented to him during the following afternoon by D'Avalon. Duke and Cream were present. Biggin quickly grasped all the implications. And his reaction was enthusiastic.

'Cor, mate,' he told Duke as they left the company office, 'this is actors' work. Once I went on the stage so's to earn a tightener, so it won't be new to me, see. It happened when I had me fruit barrer at Wapping and blimey when I thinks . . . '

When they left for El Tula's, Biggin was telling them of some other personal experience.

He was still talking when they entered the wine shop, but there he obeyed Duke's request for him to pipe down.

That morning a large caravan of seventy camels had arrived in Dana Talani from Algiers and the northern coast. All day there had been fierce haggling in the market place and now El Tula's was crammed full of Arab merchants. They still argued over their coffee or wine, and samples of goods were offered and examined on the tables.

By luck they were able to sit at the same place as on the previous night. Duke ordered a single bottle of *vin ordinaire* between them. They had a hunch they'd need to keep clear heads.

They had been there for nearly an hour when Rakal appeared. He paused impressively in the doorway and smiled when he saw them. Finding a chair, he carried it over and sat down. He seemed glad that Biggin was there.

'So you found another comrade,' he said softly.

Duke nodded.

'He's English and he wants to get out of this lousy army as much as we do.'

'It is excellent . . . you will finish your wine and then leave with me.'

Duke regarded Rakal steadily.

'You mean we're leaving right now?'

'But certainly. I told you all would be ready tonight.'

Duke said: 'Let's get this right. We wanta quit, but we also wanta know where we're quitting to. You said we'd have to work to earn this service of yours. What sort of work is it? And where? And how much dough do we get when it's all over?'

Rakal leaned back in his chair. The thin

smile was still on his lips. But only on his lips.

'You have nothing to fear. Just think my man — would we go to the trouble of getting you away from the grip of the Legion if we did not need you badly? And if we need you badly it is obvious that we must treat you well.'

Duke wasn't so convinced about that. But he put up a pretence of agreement.

Rakal added: 'Obviously I can't give details while we are still here. But I'll satisfy your curiosity to some degree. You'll be taken to a place where an enterprise of vast importance is taking place. There, being trained soldiers, you will act as guards over the labour. You will be employed thus for about six months. At the end of that time each of you will receive the equivalent of five hundred francs in any currency you choose. Your passage to your homes will also be arranged for you. The only condition for this is that of your silence — now, and afterwards.'

Biggin gave Rakal a sharp, calculating glance.

'I'll be silent, not 'arf I won't,' he said.

'I'll stand on me bloomin' 'ead to get back 'ome.'

Rakal might not have been so convinced if he had been looking at Biggin at the time.

Duke decided to have another try.

'You say we'll be guards over some sort of labour. Just what sort of work is going on that's so all-fired important?'

Rakal pulled out his platinum case from the folds of his robes and gave them each a cigarette. Then he said: 'I'm afraid that must wait, but you will know the answer very soon. Surely you'll appreciate that I cannot go into such details here in Dana Talani while sitting practically under a Legion garrison? I'm already running a great risk as it is.'

Obviously he was not prepared to say any more. He watched them finish their wine. Then he rose and said:

'You will follow me. Keep me in sight, but do not make it look as though you are with me.'

He gave them a brief bow, then his powerfully built figure swept through the door. A few moments later Duke led the others after him. The front of El Tula's wine shop gave out on to one of the main streets of Dana Talani. But even this was no more than a narrow lane according to western standards. Darkness had fallen but Arab stalls were still set along each side, leaving no more than a few feet of space in the centre down which pressed a constantly moving throng of people on foot, on mules, and occasionally on camels.

In the midst of that throng it might have been difficult to have followed a smaller man that Rakal, but his size and the richness of his robes made him conspicuous.

He strode quickly through the crowds, pushing many of them aside. None of the Arabs protested. There was something about Rakal that did not encourage protests. But soon he turned off into one of the myriad of alleys. Here it was quieter. They followed him at a distance of ten yards.

They moved thus for several minutes, switching from one alley to another until they reached the northern outskirts of the town. There Rakal stopped outside a low built mud hovel. He waited for them to come up and indicated the hovel entrance.

'You will go in there,' he said, 'and get rid of those uniforms. Do not ask questions. Do as I say. There is not much time.'

They crawled into the place on their knees. Rakal waited outside. It was a typical Arab hovel. Its main characteristic was its stink. The rank odour of years of decaying food rose from the mud floor. A primitive oil lamp burned from the ceiling. It showed that the tiny place was furnished with a few filthy and verminous skins and little else. An equally filthy Arab was squatting in a corner. He regarded the legionnaires without much interest. Then he inclined his head towards a pile of robes, which lay behind them. Obviously they were intended to put those on.

Rakal's voice came to them through the narrow opening.

He said: 'Take off your uniforms entirely before you put on the robes. And do not delay.'

The robes were anything but inviting. But they had little choice in the matter. With difficulty in the confined space they made the change, but left their Legion identity discs suspended round their necks.

And while they were doing so Duke's brain was humming.

Their orders had been to report all they could to D'Avalon as soon as they could. But in fact they now knew very little more than they had known the previous night. Should they now make a break for it and return to the barracks? Duke was certain it would be wrong to do so. No useful purpose would be served. On the other hand Rakal, and his organisation would be driven under cover as a result of the warning. But if they went on with the bluff would they ever be able to get away? That was the problem. Duke wasn't sure he knew the answer.

When Rakal's voice asked urgently: 'Are you ready?' Duke made his decision. They would carry on.

Leaving their uniforms inside, Duke led the way out of the hovel and into the comparatively sweet night air.

By now a half moon had risen. Under its light Rakal looked at them carefully. He seemed satisfied. They would pass easily as Arabs.

'We'll now walk together,' he told them, 'but do not talk.'

Again they moved through the alleys until they had passed the last of the hovels and were on the fringe of the open desert. Rakal pursed his lips and gave a low, yet penetrating, whistle. There was a soft thudding sound. Out of the gloom an Arab appeared. He was mounted on a camel and he led three other animals on a long halter.

Rakal motioned the legionnaires into a group around him.

'I leave you now,' he said. 'From now on this man is your guide. You will go with him and do as he says. You are fortunate, my friends, for on this night you have said farewell to the Legion.'

He turned. There was a rustle of robes. Then he had disappeared into the night.

Duke's throat was dry with nerve strain as he mounted one of the camels. He watched Cream and Biggin do likewise. Then they moved away fast towards the northeast.

⋆ ⋆ ⋆

And in the commandant's office at the barracks Major Pylo and Captain D'Avalon waited.

They waited all through the night until the sun was creeping over the edge of the horizon.

It was then that Pylo passed a weary hand across his brow.

'They have not been able to return,' he muttered. 'I hope we were not wrong in letting them do this work.'

D'Avalon chewed at the end of his cane.

'We can only hope,' he said. 'If indeed we were wrong, *mon ami*. I fear for our future when the general staff hear about it . . .'

6

The Mines of Hell

Three and a half days. More than eighty hours. That was the time they spent crossing the desert.

From dawn to long after sunset they pressed their camels on, enduring as best they could the vicious heat and the dry, choking sand.

At night they slept in the open without even a crude tent to cover them, at the mercy of the chill winds.

And during all that time their guide scarcely spoke a word to them, beyond saying his name was Aba. Often Duke tried to induce him to talk, but his only answer would be a shrug of his shoulders and perhaps a single meaningless word.

Thus it was almost with feelings of relief that on the morning of the third day they saw far off the blue peaks of the Atlas Mountains. These, they knew, must be their destination.

It was in the mid-afternoon that they reached the foothills and started to climb away from the desert heat. Here they began to see signs of vegetation in the form of cactus plants.

And it was here, too, that they were halted for the first time.

They were moving slowly up a narrow pass that was bordered by great walls of rock on either side when four Arabs suddenly appeared ahead of them. The Arabs were armed with aged carbines, which they raised to their shoulders. Aba spoke to them in a strange dialect and they were allowed to pass.

A little later, they dismounted when on a flat stretch of upland. For practically the first time Aba spoke to them. He did so in orthodox Arabic, which Duke could follow

'The camels can travel no further,' he said. 'But soon we will have horses.'

The camels were left tethered together, apparently to be picked up later, and they climbed on foot. If it had not been for their aching limbs after such a long period of riding they would have found the exercise almost pleasant. The cool air of the mountains was like nectar.

Duke tried to grin at the guide.

'You sure have things organised here,' he said.

Aba did not answer. They mounted the horses and rode on up the tracks.

Like most legionnaires stationed in this area of Morocco, Duke had often seen the Atlas Mountains — but only at a distance He knew that the great range was noted not only for the heights it attained, but also for its length, extending as it did for 1,500 miles through Morocco and Algeria to Tunisia. Except for a very few trading routes through it, the range was largely unexplored. But through centuries its foothills had served as hiding places for rebels and others who feared for their lives.

After an hour of horse riding along twisting passes and roughly marked tracks they came upon an unexpected spectacle. Before them was a lush, fertile valley. Grass dominated it and there were areas of semi-tropical flowers. It was obvious that this place had a rich indigenous soil, which was fertilised by regular mountain rainfall. But the valley was not all that they saw. Before them, nestled in the depth of the declivity, was something far more astonishing.

They looked upon what seemed to be a complete town.

It was composed of hundreds of small houses — or what looked like small houses. At that distance it was impossible to observe the details of them. However, they appeared to be constructed of stone and they were set apart at regularly spaced intervals.

And a little distance away from these structures the side of the valley was stripped bare, as though by explosive blasting.

All the vegetation there had been ripped away over an area of several hundred square yards and a huge opening had been driven into the side of the valley. They could just discern long lines of people moving in and out of the opening.

Cream looked at the scene in abject

amazement. Then he rolled his eyes at Duke.

'Ah'd sure like to know just what this is,' he muttered.

Duke said: 'It can only be one thing and that's a mining encampment. That's the mine entrance at the side of the valley.'

Now they were riding down the slope towards the buildings. A further hour and they were level with the nearest of them. There was no doubt that they were homes of a sort. They were of heavy limestone and the roofs were crudely constructed from wood. Arab women and children sat outside them.

There was something odd, too, about those women and children.

They just sat.

That was all. They did not talk to each other. The children did not play. They sprawled about and there was an unhealthy, helpless look about them.

Biggin pressed his horse level with Duke. He said in an awed kind of voice: 'Blimey! What's up with them?'

Duke shook his head.

'I don't know, but there's something mighty strange going on here . . . you know, this place has a funny sorta atmosphere about it . . . like approaching death.'

The three fell silent again. Duke had summed it up. The place did suggest some imminent and final tragedy.

The guide took them past the stone houses and to a large wood hut, which was surmounted by four smaller huts. It was here that they dismounted. The hut door opened and three men came out.

They were dressed European fashion in shirts and riding breeches. Each had a pistol in a holster at his waist.

They were white men.

7

The secret

Duke's mind flashed back to the last interview he'd had with Major Pylo and Captain D'Avalon. He'd been told then that Zamo, the agent, had reported that white men had been seen in the desert escorting Arabs towards the Atlas Mountains. There were plenty of Arabs here and these were white men! Therefore, in some way it seemed certain that the abandonment of the villages and the Legion desertions tied up.

One of the men came up to Duke. He was a big-boned fellow with a strong florid face out of which peeped a pair of small, shrewd, brown eyes. His dark hair was starting to grey. He extended a hand. Duke took it reluctantly.

He spoke with an American accent.

'My name's Toole,'' he said, and as he smiled he showed a row of rotten teeth. 'I heard you were arriving. We'd seven more of your boys come here a few days ago so I guess you won't be lonely.'

At first Duke could not speak. Neither could Cream and Biggin. To hear this East U.S. voice was almost the final blow. It was like living a nightmare.

In the end Duke said quietly: 'Didn't expect to meet up with another American out here.'

Toole laughed.

'I guess you didn't. But there are a whole lot of things you'll have to get used to around here. Now I want you to meet these other guys. The one with the bandy legs is Flavoni, he's an Italian. The other's called Malin and he's a Pole — but Poland don't want him any more.'

His companions nodded at the legionnaires.

Then Toole said: 'I guess you'll want some rest so I'll send you to your hut in a few minutes. But first I figure you'd like to know the pitch, eh?'

Duke said: 'We sure would. I was told that we'd have to work but we didn't figure on finding a mine in the mountains. What have you found — gold, diamonds?'

Toole laughed again. It wasn't a pleasant sound, though it was probably intended to be.

'Gee no. There's no such small time stuff here.'

He led the way into the big hut. It was well fitted out in there. A big carpet covered the floor and a polished table and several deep chairs stood around. There was even a bookcase filled with what appeared to be fairly recent volumes. A crate of whisky was in a corner. Toole went over to the crate and poured some of the liquid into glasses as they sat down. A lot of small beds were around the walls.

As he was doing so he said: 'You were contacted by Rakal. He's a good operator is Rakal. What did he tell you?'

'Only that we'd have to guard labour for six months then we'd be paid off big and set on the right tracks for home.'

Toole handed the whisky round. Duke took a long drink. It made him feel steadier.

'That was right — as far as it went,' he said. 'But there's more to it than that. We've a mighty big mining project on here. It's only just started but we've got maybe six hundred Arabs at work already and they need a lot of looking after. You see . . . some of them are already deciding that maybe they don't like this kinda toil.'

'But I guess they've just gotta stay?' Duke suggested.

'Yeah, they've just gotta stay. They'd never have a chance of finding their way through the mountains without a guide, and even if they did, they'd die in the desert. They know that. But they're being awkward about doing a full day's work. That's why we needed you guys. We needed tough boys to watch them and maybe belt their hides when it's necessary . . .'

Biggin sat up abruptly in his chair.

'Blimey! You mean you want us to be bloomin' slave drivers?'

'Maybe that's what it adds up to. But guys like you ain't gonna worry about that. Not when you'll have plenty of dough and your freedom at the end of it . . . of course, if you do wanta act like fancy pants you'll get nothing, except maybe a slug between your eyes. So I guess you'll act sensible, eh?'

Duke drained the whisky. Toole poured him some more and he was glad of it. Then he put the question he'd been waiting to ask.

'How did you get all these Arabs to come here? They're here in whole families.'

Toole sat himself on the corner of the table and dangled his legs. Duke had the strong impression of a man without any feeling, without any mercy.

'It wasn't so hard — not when we pitched the proposition right. You see, we selected three small villages where they don't have much contact with the outside world. We told them there was big dough waiting if they'd do a few weeks mining work here and they'd be looked after good. We made it seem fine. Nearly all the men agreed right away.'

Duke could understand that. The Arabs of the remote desert villages were notoriously simple. They were capable of believing almost any story. That was why in the past unscrupulous leaders had been able to organise them against the Legion.

But Duke wasn't satisfied. He asked: 'Yeah, I guess the men would fall for that. But women and kids ain't much use. How did you get them to come and why?'

'That was kinda easy, too. Most of the men wanted their families with them and so did we. You see, bud, we wanted those villages cleaned right out so there was no one to start squawking about what had happened. There's not much chance of interference here, but we can't afford any risks. In the end they all agreed to come because the few who wanted to stay behind would have stayed on their own. Get me?'

Duke got him. He analysed the information quickly. It completely bore out the reason for the abandoned villages and Zamo's story.

Cream said: 'It musta been a big job gettin' all those folks across the desert, mister.'

Toole looked almost contemptuously at the big man.

'Not so big. Most of them rode on mules. And we chose villages which were not so far from the mountains.'

Biggin stood up. The Cockney eased over to the whisky bottle and poured himself a big measure. There was nothing bashful about Legionnaire Biggin. Then he said: 'Listen, mate, once I was in business myself. Not 'arf I wasn't. So I knows a thing or two. And one of them is that there's a big organisation behind this and you're not the boss, see?'

Toole gave out one of his mirthless laughs.

He said: 'You're smart for a Limey. Sure — I'm only the local boss. But what I say right here goes, so don't make any mistake about that, bud. And there is something big behind me and behind this whole outfit . . . it's an association of wise guys with enough dough and enough nerve to use what we've found here to hold the whole world by the neck.'

Duke's brain was quivering on the verge of the answer as he asked: 'What have you found?'

Toole answered smoothly: 'Uranium . . . the stuff that kicks off atomic power.'

8

Dark Depth

It was more than a mere silence that followed. It was a period of stunning and deathly realisation. Here in the Atlas Mountains was being secretly worked one of the earth's rarest and most dangerous minerals. A mineral, which, in the wrong hands and in sufficient quantity, could be sold to unscrupulous governments with possibly ghastly results.

No wonder then, that they need secretly to mobilise labour. And needed other desperate men to watch over that labour.

If the Legion command were to know that this was the reason for the abandonment of villages and for the desertions . . .

It would immediately be an international matter. Coded telegrams would hum between all the great capitals of Europe and beyond. Certainly a powerful

Legion task force would be ordered into the mountains to seize the workings pending high level decisions.

But would the Legion command ever get to know. Duke felt sickened as his mind probed the prospects.

Toole had been right when he said they could not find their way out of the mountains without a guide. And beyond the mountains there was the heat and horror of the Sahara. The situation seemed hopeless. They were trapped. They who had been sent to get just this vital information had at one and the same time succeeded and failed.

Toole broke in. It was as though he understood Duke's thoughts.

'You don't feel so good about it, uh? You feel maybe you'd like to quit. Well, the seven others who came before you felt the same way when they got the detail. But they saw reason. They saw there was nothing they could do but stay here. After all, it ain't such a bad prospect. Six months from now you collect a whole lot of dough and you're free men.'

Duke took a firm hold on his emotions.

There was nothing to be done right now except to go on bluffing. And he had to give the lead to Cream and Biggin.

'I guess you're right,' he said. 'It's only that this is all kinda bigger than we thought. But what you do with the uranium ain't our concern so long as we're treated right and paid off the way you said.'

Toole looked pleased. He said he thought they'd take it like that.

Then he added: 'Maybe before you rest up you'd like to take a look-see at the mine. You'll be down there seeing the Arabs don't take too many rests while they work. They're showing a tendency that way and I figure it's because the place ain't too healthy when you're right on top of the seams. But that won't worry you guys. You won't be close enough for it to affect you.'

He moved out and they followed, Flavoni and Malin bringing up the rear.

Before they started for the mine entrance Toole took Duke's arm and pointed to three nearby points on the surrounding peaks. Duke hadn't noticed them before, but now he made out what seemed to be minor fortifications.

'We have machine guns up there,' he said. 'They're manned day and night by my personal staff of Europeans. It's just in case any of the Arabs down here start getting too rough to handle easy.'

Duke said: 'It looks like you've got a big staff of white folks.'

He nodded.

'Yeah, around twenty of them. But most are chemists like myself. That's another reason why we needed you boys so urgently.' He indicated the smaller huts. 'Those are the laboratories where the stuff's tested and cased for transport. That's quite a job the transport to and from here. We use the route you came here on, but up till now we've only been bringing equipment into the place. The first of the uranium won't leave for a few days yet.'

Cream had been listening closely. From his great height he looked down on Toole and asked: 'If you wanted more guards why didn't you enlist more from the place you got the chemists, mister?'

Toole didn't seem to mind answering.

'Because it ain't easy to get the sort of guys we wanted. Tough guys that we could rely on for this kind of work. But we figured a few legionnaires would fit exactly and it seems we were right.'

By now they were at the mine entrance. There was a two-way traffic of Arabs. One line was going into the mine. The other was coming out. Those leaving were staggering under the load of baskets of rock, which they were depositing in a mound.

Duke gave out an involuntary gasp as he got a close view of those Arabs. The sight made him feel sick. All of them seemed to have lost their natural dark copper colour. They were a dingy grey. And large sores had opened on their hands and faces.

'Jeeze . . . what's happened to them?'

Toole wasn't concerned.

'It's the radioactivity. We don't have protective clothing out here. It ain't possible to have all the refinements. Like I said, uranium's funny stuff when you're working close to it.'

Duke knew now why the Arab women had been silent and deathly as they sat outside their homes. They were watching their men being slowly killed.

Biggin suddenly stopped dead. The pallor on his face almost matched that of the Arabs.

'Governor — I'm not working in that mine,' he said firmly. He'd put into words exactly what Duke and Cream had decided.

Toole remained composed.

'You don't have to. Your work'll be to stand around here and check the amount of rock each of the Arabs brings out. We've got an easy system for doing that and it's what the other Legion guys are doing right now. They're working just inside the entrance.'

They followed into the mine.

The entrance was little more than a cave and Duke thought it probable the deposits had only been discovered because by some fluke of nature it was so easy to get at them.

It made a gentle slope downwards and oil lamps were let into the high walls at intervals. Some boxes of explosives for blasting were stored at the side.

It was then that they saw Legionnaire Goetler and the six other deserters.

They were dressed in rough slacks and singlets. Two of them were holding pencils and paper pads and appeared to be checking the Arabs as they went in and out. The others were keeping the wretches in line and occasionally pushing them forward. All of them stopped this work as they noticed the new arrivals.

Goetler came hesitantly forward. He looked tired. He didn't look the same sort of man that they had seen that night in El Tula's. There was almost an expression of shame about him.

He said: 'I heard some more were coming . . . but I didn't think it would be you.'

Duke didn't answer. Neither did Cream nor Biggin. There just didn't seem to be any sort of answer.

Toole said: 'I'm gonna leave you guys together now. Goetler will give you all the help you want. Work for the day will be finishing in a minute.'

He strode away with Flavoni and Malin.

There was ice, sheer ice, in Duke's voice as he said to Goetler: 'We've got a whole lotta things to talk about, bud.'

★ ★ ★

Toole poured himself another whisky. Then he looked round him with distaste. In addition to Flavoni and Malin several others of the European staff had arrived in the hut. They sprawled about on the chairs and beds, relaxing now that the working day was over. It was at this time every day that Toole felt the greatest dislike for his colleagues. It amounted almost to a sense of revulsion.

'Scum!' he thought savagely. 'Miserable scum! They are worse than those wretched Legion deserters.'

True, they were all talented men, these chemists and technicians who composed his staff. That was what made it worse. In a score of devious ways they had ruined their lives. They were men without background, probably without honour.

They had been glad to accept this work. Glad to accept the months of isolation in the mountains, indifferent to the great betrayal in which they were involved, so long as they received their reward.

And he, Toole, was no different in that respect from any of them. Toole faced the fact and to himself he admitted it. His years of training, of sheer sweat, had resulted in this . . . In skulking on the fringe of the Sahara while involved in an enterprise that was a danger to all humanity.

Toole was indeed among the most unhappy of men when he was in this mood — the mood when he was loathing himself, and the others, for lack of scruples.

His eyes drifted towards Flavoni, the fat Italian with the bowed legs. The organisation had found Flavoni in Casablanca. He'd been leading an inconspicuous life here — and for a good reason, no doubt. It was whispered that since the recent world war the governments of several countries would be interested in interviewing Flavoni. Still . . . in many respects he was a useful man. Not only good at his work, but he'd shown himself adept in other matters. For example, he knew the route through the mountains well and had several times acted as an emergency guide.

That reminded Toole. He swallowed the last of his whisky. Then he said:

'Flavoni, tomorrow you'll be going out with three others to a village by name of Drura. The Arabs there have been softened up and they're rarin' to work here. You'll bring them in.'

Flavoni did not look pleased. The prospect of days in the desert was one that he would have preferred to avoid. He told Toole so.

'Me — but why me? You have other guides, haven't you! What about Aba, or that man Rakal?'

Toole had expected this. He decided to deal with Flavoni the hard way. In Flavoni's case, the hard way consisted of humiliating him before the others. He was a proud man, was Flavoni.

'Aba needs a rest. He's been in the desert for months and I'm gonna let him lay up here for a while. Rakal's been at work in Dana Talani and he's bringing in the next lot of Legion deserters himself. He's expected tomorrow. He'll need a rest, too. But you're okay, Flavoni, only you've got too much fat on you. Maybe a little job like this'll help you lose some of it, eh?'

A few of the others laughed. Toole joined them. There were tears of fury in the Italian's eyes.

*   *   *

And at Dana Talani . . .

Major Pylo took the evening parade himself that day. This was unusual, for he normally left that task to one of his junior officers. The decision had been taken on the spur of the moment. Pylo thought that perhaps while he was out on the barrack square his mind might become clearer. He had been in a muddle all day. The worst sort of muddle. The sort that arises out of indecision. Perhaps a break with his usual routine might help.

As he walked down the ranks of men Pylo assessed the situation. He mentally numbered off the salient facts that had developed in the last few days since the two Americans and the Englishman left.

Un . . . that Arab, Rakal, had at first continued to appear in the wine shop.

Deux . . . the other night five more legionnaires had deserted. Since then Rakal had not been seen.

Trois . . . nothing had been heard from the three legionnaires who had deliberately offered themselves as deserters.

Three vital and depressing facts!

With D'Avalon and Sergeant Collat behind him, Major Pylo went automatically through the processes of inspecting a parade. Occasionally he would pause to adjust part of the equipment of some legionnaire. In one case, in which the man had allowed a few grains of sand to remain in the breech of his Lebel, Pylo turned on him a blistering sentence of reprimand. Then he told Collat to take a note of the legionnaire's name and number . . .

But all the time Pylo's mind was grappling with other matters.

What ought he to do?

There had been no word from the three legionnaires. Obviously, they had been unable to send a message. Therefore something must have gone wrong. Seriously wrong. Would it help matters to send out a message giving the facts to all garrisons in the Morocco command? Up to now he'd avoided doing this because the lives of those three men might well depend on absolute secrecy.

There was another thought at the back of his mind. A nagging and unpleasant thought that he'd tried to subdue. But it was becoming stronger. As they left the parade ground he turned to D'Avalon and said: 'Come to my office. There are matters I wish to discuss.'

Pylo did not go behind his desk. Instead he looked moodily through the window, across the square, and at the narrow streets beyond. He said: 'I'm wondering . . . might those three men have been tempted?'

D'Avalon gave a tight smile.

'You mean — might they have decided to desert properly, instead of merely making a pretence of doing so?'

'*Mais oui*. I used the word 'tempted' advisedly. It would be a great temptation, would it not?'

D'Avalon strolled over and stood beside the Major. They both looked out of the window.

'I don't think it would be a temptation to those men,' D'Avalon said. 'You see, desertion only appeals to the desperate or the stupid. Those men are neither. Furthermore, they would not cheat us. Of that I am sure, for they are men from my own company and I know them.'

He spoke firmly and Pylo seemed to be convinced.

'Then I think I'd better send out a general alarm to all units, giving details of what they have been doing. At the moment, if they fall into the hands of some of our more remote garrisons they may well be shot as deserters, for they have nothing to prove their story. Most of the messages can go out by coded radio. I'll have that attended to immediately. But there are one or two places without radio . . . '

D'Avalon finished the sentence for him.

'Such as Fort Ducane and Fort Ney.'

'Yes, I was thinking of those two in particular. They will have to be informed by personal message, so you will go on your expedition into the desert after all, *mon ami*.'

D'Avalon sucked the end of his cane. He looked thoughtful.

'It is not the sort of expedition I first planned,' he said. 'Now I will be no more than a porter with a message. I suppose I'd better make for Fort Ducane first. It is nearer . . . but isn't that man Major Dvan the commandant there?'

In spite of his fatigue and anxiety, Pylo chuckled.

'*Oui*, no other! You know of Major Dvan, then?'

D'Avalon groaned.

'I have met him. He is without doubt the most objectionable fool in the Legion. I'll try to make my visit to his fort as brief as possible . . . '

9

Tell the Legion

The ten legionnaires were billeted together in a hut. It was better accommodation than they ever saw during their service. It was furnished almost as well as Toole's own hut and it was nearly as big. But at the moment there was an uncomfortable atmosphere in the place. In fact, it was more than uncomfortable. It was crammed with static emotion.

Duke, Cream and Biggin had taken off their robes and had put on slacks and singlets. Duke had lighted a cigarette from a big box on the table and he was watching Goetler through the smoke.

Goetler was sitting on his bed, trying not to look at Duke. But the pretence of indifference wasn't kidding anybody.

The crisis started to develop when Duke said: 'We can't go through with

86

this. None of us can.'

Goetler had his eyes cast towards the floor when he answered.

'We've got to,' he said. 'And I'm interested in what's at the end of this work. That's what I came here for.'

Duke gave out a curse under his breath. It was a single, comprehensive word.

'Interested in what's at the end of it! Are you crazy? Do you think these bums'll ever let us outa here alive? If you do, let me set your mind at rest. They won't. They won't pay us off, except maybe with a slug in our backs.'

Now Goetler looked up. So did most of the others.

'What do you mean? Why shouldn't they keep their bargain? That uranium must be making them a fortune.'

Duke dragged deep on the cigarette before replying. He wanted to pick his words carefully. He knew the material he was trying to convince. Knew that among that hotchpotch of nationalities he had to put his arguments with crystal clarity or the points would surely be missed.

Goetler . . . he was of rather more than average intelligence. But the others with him were certainly not.

'Of course they'll make dough,' he said. 'I figure they must be counting on getting hold of millions of dollars through this find. Particularly since they'll have practically no labour costs. But do you think they're gonna let guys like us out into the world when it's all over so we can shoot our mouths off? No sir, they won't do that. They aren't dumb.'

They had understood. One or two of the legionnaires even grunted in a kind of uncertain agreement.

Goetler said: 'That's a risk we've got to take, isn't it? We can't do anything about it. We can't get out of this place.'

Duke threw down the cigarette and stamped on it. Then he moved towards Goetler. The Pole stood up as he approached. He flinched as Duke gripped him hard on the shoulder.

'I figure we've just gotta get out. We got in, didn't we? We have to get a message to the Legion about what goes on here. We must tell the Legion somehow!'

Goetler's rough-hewn face paled slightly. There was astonishment in his eyes as he spoke.

'Tell the Legion! We're deserters, aren't we? Even if we could do that, what would happen to us for our trouble? Now let me tell you something, you stupid American. We'd all be shot. That's what would happen. Shot. We'll just have to take our chance here and Toole and the rest of them know it. From the moment we deserted we were entirely in their hands, my friend.'

Duke turned away. He didn't want Goetler to see his face. He knew the Pole was right. Terribly right. He blamed himself for attacking the subject so openly. Temporarily, he had forgotten that although his life and that of Cream and Biggin were safe so far as the Legion was concerned, those of the others were not.

'That ain't definite,' he said. 'This information we have is big. Very big. The Legion might think twice about executing guys who risk their necks to reveal it.'

It was a weak argument and Duke knew it. So did Goetler. He seized on it.

'Very well . . . suppose our lives are spared, what then? Twenty years in a French tropical penal colony for us. Twenty years at least. Perhaps life. That would be our most generous reward and I don't want it.'

Duke looked desperately around him. Among those who had deserted with Goetler there was not one sympathetic face. These were men who had been ground down almost to the level of animals by a merciless military discipline. That was why they had quit. Right now, they were living comfortably. Perhaps they did not like the work they had to do. But they had easily overcome that distaste.

Probably, too, they did not understand the significance of the mineral that they were helping to mine. All they knew was that they personally were all right at the moment and they stood a chance of having money and freedom. No argument to the contrary would convince such men.

Duke went back to his bed and sat on the edge of it. He felt defeated. He was defeated. Cream gave him a grin and passed him another cigarette.

Suddenly it became Goetler's turn to move across the floor. He stopped a few inches from Duke. There was a dark and perplexed look about his features. He spoke with slow care.

'And why do you want to get away so bad? You wanted to desert, didn't you? It seems strange to me that as soon as you find what's happening here you decide you'd be better off facing a Legion court martial It seems very strange, my friend.'

It was a bad moment. For the second time in a few minutes Duke realised that he'd not only overplayed his hand, but he'd also played it too fast.

A suspicion was gathering in the Pole's mind. Most likely it was as yet an unformed suspicion, but it was there. Somehow it had to be allayed.

It was Biggin who retrieved the situation. The quick-witted Cockney moved smoothly into the breach.

'We don't want to go running to the Legion in person,' he said. 'Blimey, we ain't fond of suicide either, mate. But we think maybe if we got out of here we could escape on our own and then get word abaht what goes on in this happy valley.'

He spoke in a mixture of terrible French and his native Cockney. But Goetler understood. He seemed satisfied and went back to his bunk.

A silence fell on the hut and one or two of the men went to sleep.

It was half an hour later that Duke said in a voice that could be clearly heard by any who were awake: 'As we're gonna have to take our chance in this place I guess we might as well get to know it better. How's about a walk around before we hit the hay.'

The three left the hut and went out into the night.

They walked in the direction of the Arab dwellings. When there was no chance of being overheard Duke said: 'Somehow, in some way, we've gotta get information out of this valley. We've just gotta get it to the Legion. If we don't all hell can break out in a few months when enough of that stuff has been mined.'

Neither Cream nor Biggin answered

and Duke knew why. It was one matter to say they'd got to get information out, but it was another to know how they were to do it.

They were trapped in the valley. They were prisoners without guards — but prisoners just the same. The bars to their prison were the unknown and dangerous passes which led out of the Atlas Mountains, and the blistering desert wastelands beyond. Without knowledge, without preparation, it would be impossible to get away. Right now, there was no prospect of either.

They were still quiet and thinking sullenly when they reached the nearest of the Arab dwellings. Those dwellings were now shrouded in dim, moon-pierced light and there was no one to be seen around them. All the Arabs were sleeping away some of the exhaustion of the day and forgetting the further torture which was to come on the morrow.

Occasionally from within one of the crude homes they heard a grunt or a whimper from some sleeping man. The place was an epitome of misery.

Biggin cleared his throat. He was about to say something, but he didn't do so. His words were arrested by the sight of a thin, bent figure leaving one of the nearest dwellings. He crawled out of the low open doorway, his soiled robes gathered tight around him. When he stood upright the moon illuminated his dark features.

It was Aba the guide who had brought them through the desert and mountains. And his face was contorted with misery.

For a few seconds he stood opposite them but did not seem to see them. His lips were trembling and there was sweat on his brow despite the coolness of the night.

Instinctively, the legionnaires stopped too.

It was sheer contrast that surprised them. The contrast between the guide who had brought them here and the man they were looking at now. Before, he had been expressionless and without emotion. He had scarcely even spoken to them. So much so, in fact, that Biggin had dubbed him 'The Robot'.

But now he was as a person whose entire self-control had all but passed away. A person who has been shaken and broken by some impact of fate.

Duke took a step towards him. Calling on his sketchy knowledge of Arabic he said: 'You are in trouble?'

For the first time the guide seemed to notice them. Without yet being an elderly man, he was past the best of his life. He turned a lined brown face at Duke. Then he fluttered a thin hand towards the dwelling from which he had just emerged.

He made several attempts to speak before the words finally emerged. And when they did they were delivered in no more than a hoarse croak.

He said: 'Ah Allah . . . it is my brother . . . I find him in there. He works in the mine . . . '

Duke came to a quick decision. Obviously at the moment the guide was incapable of saying much that was coherent. But the glimmerings of a possible plan were evolving in Duke's mind.

He put a hand firmly on his elbow and led him away. The man came without resistance. He walked with them as in a dream.

They stopped when they were on an open stretch of land. Then Duke said: 'You'd better tell us about it. Maybe we can help.'

Aba told them. The words came now in such a misery-laden torrent that at times Duke had trouble in following them. But in the end he understood and so did Cream and Biggin.

All his life had been spent as a guide across the Atlas Mountains. He knew almost every mile of them in this area. It was he who, two years before, had found the valley and the mine. Thinking the strange, dark rock in there might contain some precious metal he took samples to white traders on the coast. Soon he was persuaded to escort them to the place.

With the promise of great reward, he'd helped in moving equipment secretly into the valley and guided other white men there.

A few months before he had told his brother of the findings and the brother had immediately volunteered to work in the mine. The offer, of course, had been accepted and he was one of the first labourers to arrive, having spent the interval in the desert.

'I find my brother dying,' Aba moaned. 'I did not know . . . but there is evil in the mine which slays those who toil in it and the white men care not . . . '

The ideas in Duke's mind were collating and forming a coherent shape. But the key to them all was Aba. With the help of Aba something might yet be done. Without him nothing was possible.

Using the simplest phrases, he explained to the Arab guide what was being worked in the mine and why his brother, like all the others, was ill. Aba seemed to understand for he nodded vigorously.

Then Duke added: 'Our only hope is to get word to the Legion. You can guide us out of here Aba and you must do so.'

Suddenly the deep, retching breathing of Aba seemed to cease as his mind took in the proposal. It appeared to stagger him.

'You speak with madness,' he said. 'Yes, I could guide you, but for how far? To reach the nearest Legion post we would need much food and water as well as horses and camels. How could we get those without being seen? No, it is not possible. Nought can be done.'

Duke told him: 'When we came here we left our camels on the foothills. They must have a grazing ground in the foothills so they can easily be picked up — they are no problem.'

Reluctantly, Aba admitted this.

'But horses and food would still be needed — the horses for the first part of the journey. How would you get those?'

There was a faint suggestion of weakening in his tones. Duke seized on it. He pointed towards the Arab dwellings.

'You have seen what is happening to your own people,' he urged. 'They thought and you thought that when they came here they would gain riches and happiness. But instead they are being slowly killed. Do you not now wish to save them?'

Aba inclined his head.

Duke continued. 'Then with your help it can be done although it will be great danger for us all. Now listen to me, Aba . . . '

10

To the Desert

It was an hour later that they left Aba. He went away like a wraith in the night while they walked quickly towards the huts.

Just before they reached the huts Duke glanced at the moon and said: 'There isn't so long before it'll start to break daylight. That means we've gotta move fast. You know what to do — don't make any mistakes.'

He slapped Cream and Biggin on the shoulders and watched them for a moment as they ran silently towards the mine entrance.

Then Duke turned towards his own particular task — a task that lay inside the big hut that was occupied by Toole and his staff.

It was a roughly built structure, like all those in the valley, having been put up by the Arabs. But it was nonetheless solid.

Entrance was gained by a single large door set in the centre. Duke walked very slowly until he reached that door.

There he paused and listened. At first he could hear no sound from within. Then as his ears adjusted themselves he caught the faint pitch of heavy breathing — a lot of heavy breathing, for discounting those on duty behind the gun posts there must be more than a dozen men in there.

There was a primitive latch handle on the door. The sort that is almost impossible to operate silently. Duke closed his hand round it as though it were constructed of delicate silk. He pressed it down by nearly imperceptible degrees. There was a clicking sound from within. Not loud, but in contrast to the quiet it seemed loud enough. He froze still. There was a grunt from inside as one of the occupants turned over. That was all.

Then Duke pushed on the door.

It opened silently for the first few inches. Then it creaked. A breeze blew in through the aperture and seemed to disturb some papers on the table, for there was a rustling in that direction. He pushed a little further. Then he pressed through the opening and closed the door behind him.

The first stage had gone through okay. He was in the hut. He sent up a prayer of thanks that it had not been locked.

Apparently Toole and his men were satisfied that their personal safety against the Arabs was safe in the hands of the men behind the machine guns.

Now the noise of sleeping men came to him clearly and with nerve-twisting closeness.

The next move was to visualise in his mind the exact layout of the place. That wasn't easy. He'd only been inside once before, when they'd first been interviewed by Toole.

And since the windows were small only the faintest streaks of moonlight came in. It was enough to show up a few fuzzy outlines, but nothing more.

So far as Duke could remember all the beds had been set round the walls. He wanted to establish the exact locality of the one nearest to him.

He extended his left hand sideways and groped with it. At first it did not contact anything. Then it met something metal and solid. He ran his palm along it. He'd found what he wanted.

Duke suddenly realised that he was breathing loudly — too loudly. But such was the tension it was almost impossible to control it. He told himself; 'You've gotta take this easy. You don't have to hurry . . . '

He groped upwards behind the back of the bed. There he felt a length of material, which must be hanging from a hook. Then something stiffer, more solid. It was leather.

It was a belt. He ran his fingers along the belt and as he did so he felt his vitals jump with triumph.

It was a gun belt. And the gun was in the holster.

That was what he'd wanted, what he'd risked coming in here for. They had to get at least one gun between them.

Any attempt to get out of the mountains and across the desert while completely unarmed would be crazy. That gun was the first necessity.

Before attempting to detach it from the hook Duke weighed it carefully. It was heavy. Using his other hand to grasp the holster so it did not swing he then lifted it towards him. It would have been easier to have taken the gun away on its own. but the spare shell pouches were in that belt.

He had got the equipment completely away when it happened.

There was a thud.

The coat, or whatever else had been on the hook, had fallen to the floor. Most likely it was a coat, for only articles in the pockets would account for the substantial noise. It seemed as loud as a kick on a drum.

There was a wild moment when Duke decided to rush for the door. But in almost the same instant he got his nerve back and waited.

There was a creaking sound from the bed. The man in it was waking. He grunted something that was a mixture of enquiry and surprise. Duke didn't wait any longer. That grunt had enabled him to fix the position of the man's head.

He made a wide arc with the pistol holster, aiming it at where he hoped the face would be. He was lucky. The man in the bed was not. The holster hit something soft and yielding. There was another grunt, this time softer and sharper. Then silence. Duke waited another couple of seconds to be sure that none of the others had been roused.

Then he slipped out of the door and ran towards the mine.

Cream was waiting there. He emerged out of the cavernous shadows towards Duke. His relief could be sensed rather than observed.

'Ah sure has been worried,' he said. 'Did you get a gun?'

Duke told him he had while strapping the belt and holster round his middle. Then Duke asked: 'Have you had any trouble?'

Cream shrugged his massive shoulders.

'There was one of them white guards here. I fixed him good. That guy won't be around for a long time.'

It was then that Duke noticed the guard. He was lying full length a few yards away. He was so still he might have been dead.

'Hell . . . what did you do to him?' Duke breathed.

The moon showed up Cream's deep grin.

'Ah just slugged him. But ah did it in a certain way.'

'Was he armed?' Duke asked quickly.

'Sure. He had a pistol, but ah've got it now.' He indicated the weapon.

Duke figured that so far things were going better even than he'd hoped. The possibility of there being a guard on the mine entrance hadn't occurred to him. The fact that there was one could have been a tragedy. But, thanks to Cream, it had turned out to be a stroke of fortune, for they now had two guns between them. Duke almost regretted running the risk of going into the hut, but decided that on balance it had been worthwhile.

'How's Biggin making out?' Duke asked.

'He's found the T.N.T. and he's fixin' it up right now.''

Duke said: 'Okay . . . you stay right

here and keep your ears open. I had to slug a guy too, one of those in the big hut. I figure he'll be outa action for quite a while as well. But in case anything does seem to be happening from that direction let us know right away.'

Duke went into the mine.

Biggin had lit some of the oil lamps. Duke followed them for fifty yards down the incline. There he saw the Cockney. He was dragging a small but obviously heavy wood case towards a spot where he'd piled several other similar cases. Biggin paused when he saw Duke. He wiped sweat off his brow with his sleeve.

'Listen, cock sparrer.' he said, 'have I got enough o' this bloomin' stuff out? There seems enough 'ere to blow up 'alf the Sahara.'

Biggin had plenty of reason to be exhausted. Duke nodded.

'You've done okay. There ought to be enough explosive here to seal this entrance. We won't worry about the Sahara. Did you have any trouble finding the stuff?'

Biggin said he hadn't. As they'd expected, the T.N.T. used for blasting in the mine had been stored in a recess only a little way inside the entrance.

The next move was to set a fuse to the stuff so as to block the mine. Duke knew that such a blockage would be no more than temporary. With the amount of Arab labour available, it could soon be cleared. But it would almost certainly delay transit of the first consignment out of the valley. And that was what was wanted. Delay in the valley while they attempted to get away with its secret.

Duke said: 'We'll have to use a trail of oil from the lamps as a fuse. That'll give us time to get clear if we make it long enough. Then . . . '

Cream's voice came to them. It came faint and hollow and echoed through the mine. It said: 'There's lights goin' on in the big hut. Ah think them boys have found the guy you slugged . . . '

For a second Duke panicked. He was torn between two possibilities. Should he risk laying and lighting the fuse? Or should he quit right now and stake everything on getting away?

It was a second call from Cream that decided him.

'You'd better hurry along,' Cream told them from the entrance. 'It looks to me like them boys are coming outa the hut to raise an alarm.'

There was no time to seal the mine. To attempt it would mean being trapped. Duke gestured to Biggin.

'Okay — this is where we've gotta find Aba.'

They ran towards the entrance. Cream was there, peering through the darkness. All the lights were on in the hut and the door was open. It was possible to discern silhouettes as the occupants came running out. Distant shouting reached them. But they did not stay to study the details.

Turning to their right, they pelted past the Arab homes and towards the place where they'd arranged to meet Aba. The meeting place had been fixed in a rocky declivity at the western end of the valley, near the track that led out of it. From the mine the distance was a full mile.

When they had covered two hundred yards Duke signalled for them to slow down.

'Take it at a trot,' he shouted. 'We've

gotta keep some energy for emergencies and right now none of us is in training for a marathon.'

He was right about that. They were still sore and stiff from the long ride over the desert.

They eased down to a less urgent pace. Occasionally they glanced over their shoulders, but now the huts and the mine entrance were out of sight and there was no sign yet of a chase.

If Aba met them as arranged with the horses, and if he'd been able to get food and water, then they might yet get clear.

They were halfway to the meeting place when a sudden crackling inferno of death forced them to drop flat on the ground. It forced them to remain thus while they gathered their wits.

The three machine guns had opened fire.

11

Aba the guide

They had been under fire before often enough. Sometimes even under fire from machine guns, for in recent years rebel Arab tribes had obtained automatic weapons. But they had never become used to the experience. No one ever does.

They lay on their bellies and sweated. It was the sweat of sheer fear. The fear that arises from the possibility of a hot slug — or maybe several hot slugs — twisting into one's back at any moment. There was no cover, either. That made it worse. Only the concealment of the night.

Sometimes the three guns would be firing together. At other times only one or two would be being used. But always there was hell in their venomous clatter. And it was made worse by the Arabs. They began to scream and wail and the distant sound could clearly be heard above the gunfire.

They must have been crouching for a full minute before Duke realised a vital fact. The guns were being aimed at random. Certainly no shots had passed anywhere near them. Which meant only one thing. They had not been seen and their precise position was unknown.

He raised his head and looked around. Immediately he knew that the machine guns were of an old type. Probably they had been purchased from some discarded European army issue. He knew that because the flashes as they fired could be clearly seen. Anti-flash muzzle devices had been common for many years.

And there was something else, too. The men behind the guns didn't know a lot about how to operate them. They were firing long, sustained bursts, sometimes of nearly a minute at a time. That was not only wasting ammunition, it was over-heating the muzzles. Even though they were probably water-cooled, they'd soon be rendered useless under that sort of treatment. The rifling would get red hot.

Because of his training, Duke knew

that a real machine gunner seldom fired bursts of more than five seconds — and five seconds was long enough.

It seemed that Cream and Biggin had been working things out along the same lines as Duke. They, also, were now looking around them. Cream said: 'Them boys need to take a musketry course.'

In spite of the situation, Duke grinned. They got to their feet and again started to move. Because of their dark clothing, there was little chance of their being seen in the thin moonlight. But the danger would come with the dawn.

They just had to get out of that valley before daylight or the machine guns would cut them down easily. And it couldn't be very long before dawn was due to break. None of them had a watch, but they were all certain of the fact.

By now they were climbing up a slight gradient at the side of the valley most distant from the workings. The guns were still firing, but their sound came to them faintly.

After climbing for a hundred yards they came to a dip in the ground. There, a few feet below them, was Aba. And he was holding four horses. Duke rushed down towards him. In a moment of emotion he almost embraced the guide.

'You've made it!' he gasped. 'We sure would have been in a tight spot if you hadn't been here.'

Aba now had recovered from his distress of earlier in the night. He regarded the legionnaires with something akin to his former cold detachment.

'I keep my pledge,' he announced. 'But we must not delay. The fiends in the valley are already astir and the dawn is almost upon us.'

They looked towards the eastern sky and knew that Aba was right. The stars were paler and there was a faint streak of grey over the clouds.

They made a quick check of the horses. They were small sturdy animals of the type well accustomed to mountain tracks. Each was saddled and carried a skin of water. Aba pointed to a large package on his own horse.

'I have meat for us all here,' he said.

They mounted and with Aba leading

started up the track which led out of the valley.

* * *

And when it was full daylight they were well clear of the valley and moving steadily down towards the foothills.

As they did so the temperature rose rapidly. It was the high elevation of the valley that had accounted for its temperate climate. Now they were descending towards the heat of the Sahara.

By mid-morning they emerged from a pass to a cactus-covered plain. There they counted eight camels grazing.

Aba was about to dismount and move towards them, but Duke restrained him.

'Isn't there any kind of guard on these animals?' he asked.

Aba shook his head.

'It is not necessary. Food grows for them here and there is also water. This is as far up the hills as they can come and they are always left here to await the return journey.'

Saddles and harness for the camels

were stored under some rocks. Aba fitted them and they mounted, leaving the horses to graze in their turn.

It was early afternoon and the smell of the desert sand was already in the air when they were halted by the Arab guards. They looked with some surprise at the three legionnaires and kept their carbines aimed at them until Aba said:

'All is well . . . we leave to get supplies from the coast.'

A little later the camels had the familiar sand of the desert under their feet and were striding out. The foothills and the mountains were behind them.

Duke brought his animal level with that of Aba. He shouted: 'Where exactly are we heading?'

Aba answered: 'There is an oasis twenty miles from here. We will spend the night there. Then on the morrow we will make our way to the Legion's Fort Ducane.'

Fort Ducane! That name brought back a flood of memories and not all of them pleasant. Yes, he'd been at Fort Ducane before, and with Cream.

That tough stone edifice marked the most easterly point of France's authority in Morocco. Periods of service in it were regarded with horror by legionnaires. Many stories were told (and not all were untrue) of men driven to madness and suicide by the remoteness of the place and its heat.

Duke put another question to Aba.

'When will we reach the fort? We haven't any time to waste so I was wondering whether we should try to press on overnight.'

Aba gestured emphatically with one hand as he held the saddle pommel with the other.

'That must not be attempted. Even I cannot always be sure of my way when I travel at night — particularly here, my friend, where the desert is devoid of caravan traffic. Also the camels will be tired . . . no, it is better that we rest for the night.'

Duke accepted the advice. In fact, there was little else he could do. They were almost helpless without Aba. He alone could take them to Fort Ducane, as only he had been able to lead them through the mountains.

As they rode on Duke considered the prospect of Toole sending out men after them. He decided there was little prospect of him doing that. In the valley they hadn't the men to spare for such purposes and while their own absence had been discovered before they were clear of the place, it was by no means certain that they would detect Aba's absence for some time — maybe for a day or two — as he was supposed to be resting in the valley. Therefore they'd most likely conclude that the legionnaires would be killed or lost in the mountains.

He was still brooding on the subject when Cream called to him: 'Wake up and exercise them eyes! There's the oasis right in front of us!'

Cream was right. So far away that they seemed to be pressed against the horizon, they saw a cluster of palm trees. Sensing the prospect of water and rest, the camels lengthened their stride.

It was when they were still a mile away that they saw they would not be the only travellers at the oasis. A group of robed figures could be discerned. They had set up tents beneath the trees.

Duke asked: 'Is that oasis used much?'

Aba told him it wasn't.

'It is off the usual caravan paths,' he said. 'It is indeed a strange chance which brings two parties of travellers to it on one day.'

Night was falling fast and the first hint of a cold nocturnal breeze was in the air when they rode into the oasis.

Six Arabs were there. They were eating goat meat as they squatted outside the two tents. Their camels were tethered to the trees.

In the failing light it wasn't possible to make out the details of the men who were due to be their companions.

Both groups looked with unsatisfied curiosity at each other through the gloom.

Duke was about to dismount, but a sudden sense of insecurity made him change his mind. Without being able to define it, his instinct told him that all was not well at that oasis. That there was danger here. Real danger.

Apparently the others felt the same way. They, too, stayed in their saddles.

Duke thought: 'What's gotten into me? What am I scared of?'

And he couldn't provide an answer. Not yet, he couldn't.

He looked carefully round him. There was nothing outstanding about the Arab travellers. They'd pitched tents and were eating in weary silence as any Arabs would do after a long day's trek. They were poorly dressed in the cheapest of white cotton. Even in the semi-dark he could discern that fact. All of them, judging by their garments, were in a pretty abject state of poverty.

All of them . . . except one. Except the one who was sitting a little apart from the others and staring especially hard at them . . .

This Arab was in white silk. Silk that was heavily brocaded. Around his middle there was a purple sash through which was inserted a jewelled knife.

Duke urged his camel closer to the Arab. And as he did so the Arab got to his feet.

They faced each other, Duke looking down from the saddle the other up from ground level.

He was tall and, for his race, powerfully built.

They recognised each other simultaneously.

It was Rakal. It was the man who was persuading the legionnaires to desert. And these men with him were not Arabs. They were more Legion deserters being taken across the desert to the Atlas Mountains.

Duke's right hand rushed towards his pistol holster. But Rakal halted the move. He did so by raising both his hands, palms forward, in a gesture of peace. That usual smooth confidence was still in his voice as he spoke.

'So it is the American and his comrades ... surely you are not leaving our mountain retreat?'

There was insolence there, too. It needed a lot to ruffle Rakal.

The moment they realised what had happened Cream and Biggin rode their camels up to either side of Duke. Aba dismounted and stood near to Cream.

Duke didn't answer immediately. He looked towards the deserters. They, too, were now on their feet. They stood about uncertainly in their unaccustomed robes. Then he glared down at Rakal.

'So you've got some more legionnaires who are ready to earn their freedom! But this time, Rakal, it's gonna be disappointing for you, because you ain't taking them any further, see!'

Rakal eased his shoulders and there was a rustle from his fine robes.

'You speak very foolishly . . . but I'm puzzled, how is it that you are leaving the mountains with our guide, Aba?'

'Because we don't like what goes on there, and neither does Aba. That's why he's helping us. You might as well know this, Rakal, but we're heading right for Fort Ducane and we're gonna let the garrison know just what is going on in your mountain valley. So I guess you'll be having some visitors there in the next few days — Legion visitors.'

Rakal took a step forward until he stood directly beneath Duke, There was a glitter to his eyes. An evil glitter like that of a wounded snake.

'Fool! And thou, Aba, art a traitor! We have offered you money. More money than you would otherwise see in all your lives. Then your freedom. Freedom from the army of slaves. And what do you give in return? You threaten to leave with our secret and inform the nearest French garrison. Could evil go much further?'

There was a murmur from the group of legionnaires. They saw it Rakal's way. That was obvious. They gathered round him to demonstrate their support.

Duke felt a great spasm of fury gather in his breast. He dismounted from the camel and stood within inches of Rakal. But he was speaking to the legionnaires. Duke had some of the gifts of a natural orator. He could make points forcibly and colourfully — when using his own tongue. But now, to be sure of general understanding, he had to speak in French. That was a handicap to fluency.

He told the deserters of what was being mined in the mountain valley and the condition of those who worked there.

Despite the language difficulty, he used every descriptive trick to drive home the horror of the place. Then he played his best card. The card he'd played the previous night in his argument with Goetler.

'They offer you money and freedom! Do you think they intend to give you either? I don't and that's why I quit. They wouldn't allow you to walk about with such a secret. To do so would be madness. No . . . once this work is over they'll give you a bullet . . . '

Rakal broke in. Even now he hadn't entirely lost his calm. But there was a rasping shake to his voice, which told of seething and dangerous emotions.

'He lies as all of his kind lie,' Rakal said. 'We hope soon to have three score legionnaires working in the mountains. Is it supposed we can kill them all when the task is done? To do that we would certainly have to be mighty men! In this great venture we are as much in your hands as you are in ours. All depends on a common trust. Do not be influenced because these vile and stupid men have chosen to betray that trust.'

There had been a moment when Duke sensed that he'd gained some sympathy among the deserters. His description of life in the mines had not been without effect. And even their unimaginative minds had comprehended the logic of his point that they would be murdered rather than be allowed free with the secret.

But Rakal had swayed them back. This Arab had a quick mind, which was capable of seizing on an apparent weakness in an argument and exposing it to ridicule.

Furthermore, his expert knowledge of both French and Arabic made it possible for him to insert phrases in both tongues that were easily understood by the various nationalities among the legionnaires.

Duke knew that he had taken on a more skilled dialectical opponent. But he decided to try once more. Deliberately, he turned away from Rakal so he had his back to him and was facing the deserters.

He said: 'If you go with this man you will die. Your only chance is to come with us to Fort Ducane so as . . . '

Rakal started to laugh. It was loud. It was devoid of humour. It was unpleasant to the ear. But it broke in on Duke's words and drowned them.

Duke wheeled round on the Arab. Automatically his fists had bunched. Somehow he knew that they were past the point when verbal argument would serve any purpose. Tougher and rougher measures were needed.

Cream and Biggin had got down from their camels and were moving towards him. In this sort of row Duke felt confident. The deserters would not be armed. That only left Rakal with a gun. But since Cream had gained an extra pistol, the advantage was in their favour ... four against seven, but two guns against one gun. The strength was with the side that had the most guns.

Duke's right mitt was itching. It was an almost overwhelming temptation to let go a short jab at Rakal's beard-tufted chin. But he did not do so. Suddenly he realised that no useful point would be served by having a pitched battle with Rakal and his deserters. There was another way of handling this situation. Another and more subtle way.

He moved his hand down to his holster. In a single move he unfastened the flap and had the weapon out. He aimed at the centre of Rakal's silk-encased belly. Rakal had made a fluttering movement towards his garments, as though he too were going to reach for a pistol. But he thought better of it. Duke had been much quicker.

Duke eased round so that he was again looking both at Rakal and his group of deserters. This time he spoke directly to them all.

'You are not going to the mountains,' he rasped. 'None of you are.'

The silence was disturbed only by the sound of men breathing deeply.

Then Rakal said: 'Really, my friend. Is it that you propose to keep us here at gunpoint? That would be tedious for us all, would it not!'

One of the deserters laughed awkwardly. Duke didn't join in. His face was expressionless and frozen as he answered.

'My plan is much simpler than that,

Rakal. You are coming with us to Fort Ducane. I figure they'll be interested to see you there. These other guys who're with you can come too, if they feel that way. Otherwise, I guess they'll just have to take their chance in the desert without a guide.'

Rakal rubbed the tip of a cat-like tongue along his brown lips. He almost spat out his retort.

'You can't leave these men thus. They would die.'

'That'd be their choice, wouldn't it? If they don't feel like wandering around in the desert they'd better take their opportunity of coming along with us to Fort Ducane.'

Duke heard Biggin mutter under his breath: 'You ain't 'arf being smart.'

In a different way, Rakal thought so too. Duke had made a master move and Rakal knew it. There was an air of desperation about him now. His voice had lost its smooth composure.

'I will not come with you . . . that I refuse!'

The pistol that Duke held was one of

the earlier mark Mausers with a visible striking hammer. Slowly, so that Rakal would have plenty of time to see what he was doing, Duke pulled back the hammer so as to cock the gun.

Rakal saw, all right. His eyes were fixed on that gun.

Duke said: 'I don't aim to have any trouble. Either you come voluntarily or I put a slug into you. We can't spare time for any wrestling games.'

Rakal went on looking at that Mauser for a long time. His hands were lightly thrust into his purple sash. Slowly he withdrew them in a gesture of defeat.

'Very well. I do not appear to have any choice.'

A sudden undertone of talk arose from the deserters. Harsh and ugly talk. Duke glanced towards them. This was what he'd expected. There was going to be trouble with them. That was natural. They'd just absorbed the fact that they were faced with the prospect of either being executed at the fort as deserters or dying through exposure and thirst here in the desert.

One of them pushed his way forward. Duke recognised him. He was a Bulgarian called Borola from A Company. Duke didn't know much about Borola except that he was reputed to have a murderous temper. He was a man with flattened features, small eyes, and a big jowl. It was easy to see that among his little group he was the leader. He'd established himself in that position because of his undoubted physical strength and the fact that he was never unwilling to use it. Borola was nearly as big as Cream, although his shambling movements contrasted with the black man's natural grace which is common to most trained athletes.

Borola looked evilly at Duke, then at the gun. He spat into the sand. Then he said:

'You can't kill us all, and we're with Rakal. We're not letting him go. Even if one or two of us have to be killed, we're not letting you take Rakal.'

He meant it. There was no doubt of that. And he obviously had the support of the others. Borola was fairly representative of the worst sort of bully. But he was not a coward. Contrary to the orthodox conception, bullies seldom are cowards. In fact, they are often extraordinarily brave men. Most soldiers know that. Duke knew it.

He slightly shifted his position so that his gun now directly covered the Bulgarian as well as Rakal.

Duke said slowly: 'That choice is yours, Borola. But get this right — Cream here's holding a gun, too. It won't be a matter of just one or two of you being killed. If you make trouble you'll all be cold meat . . . all of you. You know you don't have any sorta chance against two guns.'

Borola's big jowl was working. Twitching from side to side. In the semi-darkness he looked strangely like some menacing animal. As he watched him Duke thought: 'He ain't scared yet. This guy's gonna be dangerous . . . '

Maybe Borola was taking too much of his attention. Maybe Cream and Biggin should have been watching Rakal more closely. Whatever the reason, Rakal was left only semi-guarded for a few moments. And the big Arab took full advantage of them.

His right hand snaked out. It slapped against the barrel of the Mauser knocking it sideways. At nearly the same moment his other hand gripped the weapon, twisting it in an effort to pull it free of Duke's grip.

There was the smallest fraction of a second in which Duke was taken by surprise. In which his reflexes were unable to adjust themselves to the new emergency. That infinitesimal period passed when he felt Rakal pulling on the Mauser.

The Arab had unconsciously stepped close to Duke in fact, he was less than six inches away from him as he struggled for possession of the gun. Duke let him struggle. Let Rakal concentrate attention on his gun hand. Meantime, Duke's left hand went into violent action.

His fist started travelling from waist level. It moved in a slightly upward direction and it made contact over the Arab's kidney region. It was not a clean punch. It wouldn't have scored any points in a clean ring. In fact, it would most likely have led to a disqualification. But this was no time for sporting niceties. That kidney punch had an immediate and dramatic effect. Rakal gave out a hollow, sickening sort of a grunt. His knees bent forward under his robes. He started to fall.

It was that fall that killed him.

His grip was still on the Mauser. Nor was he conscious of the fact. It was a natural muscular contraction, which resulted in his hold actually getting tighter as he fell. And he dragged the gun barrel down with him so that it was pointed at his own head.

The downward pull meant that Duke's index finger was pressed against the trigger. He tried to jerk it away, but there was not time. There was a crash and a smell of burnt cordite and the slug buried itself in Rakal's head.

12

Under Arrest

Rakal had ceased to live. And during those few moments in the night-shrouded oasis it seemed as though all other activity stopped in sympathy with the man who had died.

None of the ten men there moved. They stood as though suddenly paralysed. They each looked down on the richly robed and inert figure.

Somewhere, from a long way above, a vulture screeched, as with the uncanny knowledge of those birds it proclaimed its grisly knowledge. The cold wind whispered through the palm leaves.

In that brief period they all felt alone. They all felt helpless. This sudden death in their midst, because it was so unexpected, had temporarily reduced the morale of every man there.

Biggin recovered first. He moved towards

Duke and touched him on the elbow.

'Blimey — don't waste sympathy on that bag of sheets,' he suggested with typical irreverence.

Duke nodded at the Cockney, but somehow he was unable to return his grin. Then he switched his gaze to the deserters. Most of them were still looking transfixed at what had been Rakal.

This was the moment, Duke realised, to go for them again. The moment when they were confused because their guide had been killed.

'You've gotta make up your minds,' Duke said. 'And you've gotta do it right now . . . are you coming with us to the fort? There ain't no Rakal for you to cling to now, so it seems you don't have any choice.'

They looked at him stupidly. In the bovine way of foolish men who are submerged under the weight of unfamiliar circumstances.

It seemed that they might have agreed to go to the fort and face a court martial there rather than the worse prospect of wandering across the desert until they died by meticulous and agonizing degrees.

But again it was Borola who intervened.

Borola was looking at Duke's gun. He was sniffing through his wide nostrils, as though deliberately savouring the fast fading aroma of cordite.

He said: 'We'll still take our chance in the desert. I think maybe we will be able to find our own way through the mountains to the valley for it is possible, is it not, that we may be seen by some of Rakal's friends?'

To himself Duke was bound to admit that this was a distinct possibility. There were Arab guards in the foothills. The legionnaires were already at a point very close to the start of the mountain track. They had only to proceed to the mountains, which could scarcely be missed, to stand at least some chance of being seen and assisted by the agents of Toole.

Duke shivered and he wondered why. Then he knew.

The night breeze was of greater than normal velocity. And it was colder than usual. Small eddies of sand were scurrying around their feet.

Duke told the Bulgarian: 'Then go into the desert. Do as you want, but remember that you boys had your chance. You'll feel like forgetting that fact when you're yelling for water. We're going on right now for Fort Ducane.'

Aba came up to him. The guide was tense under the strain of recent events. Drifts of hair had appeared from under the front of his turban.

'I told you before that I think it better for us to rest tonight. The camels are tired and . . . '

Duke put a hand on Aba's shoulder.

He said: 'I know that. But things have changed a lot in the last few minutes. We can't waste a second getting to the fort. Toole and his mob in the valley must be pretty jittery right now, but when they find that Rakal hasn't turned up things will start to happen. My guess is that they'll try to beat it. We don't want that. Those boys and their organisation have to be taken as a job lot.'

Aba was still reluctant. The breeze had turned into a wind and there was a rusty hue over the rising moon.

'I fear a storm is approaching,' he said. 'If you insist, then I will take you on, but it would be safer to stay in this place for the night.'

He was right about the storm. It was gathering with the swift ferocity that was typical of the desert. What had a few minutes before merely been a strong breeze was now an angry wind. The palm branches were bending under the strain and soon the entire trunks would be doing so. Yes, a storm — a sandstorm probably — was gathering.

Duke had experienced sandstorms before. So had Cream and Biggin. They knew the paralysing terror of them. Duke hesitated for a moment. But only for a moment.

'We must go on and take our chance,' he said. 'In any case, there wouldn't be much rest in this oasis with those boys around.'

He gestured towards the deserters and Aba had to nod agreement. If they stayed, a watch would have to be kept on the deserters. And they'd always be under the strain of expecting a sudden assault.

As it was, from under their borrowed turbans the deserters watched them sullenly as they remounted. They could feel the glaring intensity of six pairs of eyes on their backs as they rode out of the little oasis.

They had travelled no more than twenty yards when a second man died that night.

Unlike Rakal, he died without having a fighting chance. He died without being aware of the transition between life and death, because it happened so fast. He died from a bullet that shattered his backbone.

And he was Aba the guide.

The four had been riding abreast of each other, with Aba on the flank nearest to the oasis. Duke was next to him.

Before Aba hit the ground Duke knew he was beyond any help. He also realised what had happened and he cursed himself. Rakal would have a gun. One of the deserters must have remembered that fact and got it from under his robes.

As Duke twisted in the saddle he had his Mauser out and ready. A second shot whined from the oasis trees. This one was high. Accurate aim was difficult in the dark. They must have had luck with the shot that killed Aba.

The moon, however, was giving some light and it was just possible to make out who was doing the shooting. He was recognisable by his powerful, stocky figure. It was Borola. The Bulgarian was kneeling and steadying the pistol on one leg. The others were grouped excitedly behind him.

Duke brought his own gun up. He did so steadily and slowly. He drew a careful bead on Borola. He did not want to miss. But he never fired. It was Cream who stopped him.

Cream was getting off the camel. At the same time he said to Duke: 'You leave this to me. I'm gonna have that big boy all to myself.'

There was deadly depth to his tones. A sort of deep and utter finality. No one argued with Cream when he spoke like that. Not even Duke.

Although he had a gun, Cream had made no attempt to draw it. He started to advance on Borola almost casually. One hand was inserted into his belt and his other was in his trousers pocket. Somehow he looked like a black wraith strolling inexorably towards its victim.

Borola screamed at him: 'Stop, or I'll kill you . . . '

Cream didn't stop. He didn't answer either. He went on moving towards the man who crouched among the palm trees.

They heard Borola curse. Then he fired three tunes, quickly. They were wild shots and they passed wide of Cream.

Because the range was now less than ten yards Borola's fourth shot was more accurate. It appeared to sink into Cream's left shoulder. Anyway, Cream halted in his stride for just a second and clasped a hand to the area. Then he again started to move on the Bulgarian. And still at the same unhurried pace.

Having drawn blood, Borola seemed to lose his fear — but only temporarily. He gave out an involuntary snort of triumph. Then, with careful precision, he raised his gun so that it was aimed at Cream's head. It was impossible to tell whether the shot would, have found its mark. Impossible because it was never fired. The hammer sank forward with no more than a futile click. The chambers were empty. Borola was now holding a useless hunk of metal.

It was at that stage that Cream grinned at him. Borola saw it as the smile of the devil.

'Now ah figure we're on even terms,' Cream said. You killed that Arab when his back was turned, now you can try killin' me, but ah ain't plannin' to turn my back.'

Cream was the bigger man. Probably there was not more than a few pounds difference in weight, but Cream was noticeably taller. Borola's frame was all bulk, whereas Cream's tapered to the slim waist of an athlete. Still, on physical grounds they were not unfairly matched Borola was an exceptionally big man and an exceptionally strong one. Particularly in view of his wound, it looked as though Cream was faced with a tough time.

Borola seemed to think so too as he stood upright and prepared to close with the other. He looked confident again and he flexed his shoulder muscles. And his first move was typical. As Cream got within striking distance Borola flung the empty gun at him. It was aimed at Cream's head. It missed that mark, but it slapped against his raw and bleeding shoulder wound. Cream grunted under the searing spasm of pain. Then both his long ebony arms stretched out to grasp the Bulgarian's neck.

Borola tried to step back so as to escape the grip. But a tree was directly behind him. He pressed against it as Cream's hand fumbled then closed round his throat.

There had not been time for Borola to prevent Cream establishing the grip. The tree had hindered him. But now he used all his strength and resource in an effort to break it.

He whipped a foot up and it was aimed at Cream's stomach. It didn't land there. Cream had been expecting that. He shifted fast slightly to one side and the kick passed harmlessly by.

Then Borola grasped his wrists and tried to drag them away. The veins and capillaries of his face stood out under the strain. Borola was fighting for his life, and he knew it. But the effort was useless. It seemed that no human force could break Cream's hold. Gradually at first, then more quickly, Borola's struggles became weaker. His small eyes became larger and they stared into space.

Quite suddenly he went still and limp. Only then did Cream release his hold. The dead Bulgarian dropped at his feet.

By now Duke and Biggin had dismounted. Duke gave his gun to the Cockney telling him to watch the deserters.

Then he ran towards Cream.

Cream was pressing his shirt against the wound. Duke pulled away the material and looked at the wound. He felt a wave of relief. It wasn't serious. The bullet had grazed the flesh over the shoulder, but no more. Even the bleeding was now stopping of its own accord.

Duke tore a length off his own shirt to make a bandage.

When it was fixed they moved back to the camels. And this time they left five deserters and two who were dead under the palms of the oasis.

*   *   *

The sandstorm broke just before dawn. It came with typical suddenness. In one minute they were riding fast through strong winds. In the next they were almost submerged in a wall of lashing sand and small particles of rock.

They halted the camels and pulled them down to their knees. Then they took shelter behind the animals' bodies. While the sand forced its way through their clothing, got into their mouths, ears and eyes, Duke tried to assess the situation. It didn't give him any ground for optimism.

They had been travelling by guesswork since they'd left the oasis. Without Aba they could not be sure of the route to Fort Ducane. Duke knew it lay roughly to the north-west, but in the desert a rough calculation could be entirely useless. Over a long distance a few points off course could result in their missing their target by a score of miles.

But that was all they could do — just move on and trust to luck.

By midday the storm had reached its climax. The wind had risen to a screaming crescendo so that even the loudest shout at the closest range could not be heard. Then, an hour later, it passed with baffling abruptness, just as it had arrived. Suddenly the desert became quiet again. The gloom vanished and the hot sun broke through. And as they rose stiffly to their feet they saw that the sand had forced itself into long rolling ridges, like some thick sea. Near to them the displacement had uncovered the bones of a mule and a man who must have died of exposure at some time in the unknown past.

The camels protested as they were pulled to their feet.

They were about to mount when Biggin spoke in a tense kind of whisper. He said just one word. It was. '*Listen*!'

Faintly, they heard a familiar crunching sound, such as feet make on the sand. That sound was getting closer.

Duke pulled out his gun and so did Cream.

But they put the weapons back when they saw the cause of the sound.

Twelve men emerged from behind one of the dunes.

Twelve men who marched in single file. Uniformed men with Lebel rifles slung over their shoulders.

It was a Legion patrol.

To Duke the next few minutes were chaotic. It took him, as it took them all, a few seconds in which to absorb the fact of their luck. There was no longer any need to hope that they might stumble on Fort Ducane. It was now a certainty that they'd be taken there, for by a munificent stroke of fortune they had met up with a patrol, which must have been sent from that fort.

As soon as he realised that, Duke ran towards them, followed by Cream and Biggin. The three stood to attention before a surly-looking lieutenant. Missing out all but the most relevant details, Duke explained why they were in the desert. As he spoke the lieutenant's expression assumed an added tinge of incredulity.

In any case, Lieutenant Blum was in a

bad mood. He'd resented being sent out on this patrol by the fort commandant. It was time he was given a rest from this sort of work. It was always he who had to trudge around the desert with a handful of men. And there was no reason for it. No necessity. Except, of course, that it enabled Major Dvan to send in reports to Algeria that suggested that the place was bristling with activity. All of which might reflect credit on Dvan but did not add to the comfort of Lieutenant Blum.

And this time they'd been out in a sandstorm. Now these three legionnaires with their fantastic story. It was too much for any man to endure.

Blum braced himself when Duke had finished. All of his men had heard Duke's story. Very well, then. Now they would see how he, the efficient Lieutenant Blum, would handle the situation.

Then Blum said: '*Mon Dieu*! Never have I heard such a fantastic story! Obviously you are deserters, all three of you. Therefore you are under arrest and there will be a court martial at the fort.'

147

13

Death Sentence

Major Dvan pulled open his desk drawer and extracted a box of nine-inch cheroots. He fingered one of them fondly. Some men find solace in their dreams. Others in drink. Major Dvan found it in cheroots. Dark coloured and powerful cheroots, which he never had to share because no one else would think of smoking them. And that in itself was an economy which appealed to his small and mean mind.

He lit one of the monstrosities and blew an acrid stream of smoke at the flies, which were circling round the oil lamp. Even the flies were discouraged.

Then he considered the extraordinary report that young Lieutenant Blum had just made to him.

Three deserters picked up in the desert . . . that sort of thing had happened before, of course. But, *ma foi*, for them to tell such a story! And apparently expected it to be believed! The sun must have affected their minds.

Although, of course, two of them were Americans and the other was English. Such a combination could account for a lot.

He cleared his throat heavily, then said to Blum: 'You are sure they showed no sign of wishing to resist when you found them?'

Blum shook his head.

'*Non*. They ran towards me with this preposterous tale.'

Dvan nodded wisely.

'Obviously they thought that such bluff was their only chance. But it will avail them nothing. The manuäl militcáre is quite clear on the point. It is laid down that any officer of my rank and upwards has the power of court martial over deserters who, if the case is proven, must forthwith be executed by a firing squad. Of course. I shall not shirk my duty . . . '

He looked towards his junior for reassurance. Blum gave it to him. Blum had something in common with the major in so much as he was always ready to reassure any senior officer about anything. Dvan looked pleased. This, in fact, was the sort of situation which appealed to him.

It was the sort of situation in which he could demonstrate the virtue of decision without running any particular risk. They would be pleased at Algiers. When the general staff got his report they would certainly move his name high up in the order of seniority for promotion, for he would have struck a heavy blow at the prospect of future desertions.

Major Dvan could almost see the report he would prepare.

The first part, headed 'Circumstances,' would set out fully the facts of the case. The second and more important part, under the title 'Action Taken', would outline the court martial, his verdict, and include the precise time at which the prisoners were executed against the fort walls, as required by regulations.

Dvan said: 'We'll get it over immediately. Bring the men in.'

Blum coughed slightly through the smoke as he saluted then walked out.

In the guard room Duke had his hands manacled behind his back. So had Cream and Biggin. They sat on a bench against the stone wall and looked grimly out of the single, tiny, barred window. Through it they could just see the tip of the sentry's fixed bayonet as he stood guard outside.

They had been silent for a long time. It was the silence of shock and despair. Biggin ended it.

' 'Ow is it that the geezers 'ere don't know abaht the job we've been doing?' he asked explosively.

'It was supposed to be a secret sorta mission,' Duke reminded him. 'And I guess Major Pylo didn't expect us to end up in the region of Fort Ducane. There was no reason why he should expect that.'

Cream moved his wounded shoulder. It had been dressed in the fort first aid room, but it was still aching.

'Ah figure that means they'll believe us guys when it's too late, huh?'

151

Duke said he thought so. He didn't see that he'd do any good by trying to build up false hopes. They had no truth of the assignment they'd been given. None whatever.

They had admitted to being legionnaires and their identity discs had been found round their necks. The Legion did not waste a lot of formality on deserters. And there was only one penalty for that offence.

Duke knew — they all knew — what awaited them when a key turned in the door lock and a sergeant with six armed legionnaires strode in.

Still manacled, they were escorted across the moonlit fort yard towards the commandant's office. In there, they blinked before the unaccustomed light as they were lined up before Major Dvan's desk.

As he took in the details of Dvan's appearance Duke thought: 'Hell . . . that guy looks like a washed pig!'

It was a violent description, but not altogether inaccurate.

Dvan had one of those round and pink

faces that the sun never turned brown. It only turned a more vivid pink. The rolls of flesh seemed to cover his features, leaving only a vague impression of a snout-like nose, a half-open mouth, and a number of chins that receded into each other as though beating a portly retreat towards his big neck.

It was, however, one of those charities of nature that Dvan himself was well satisfied with his appearance. He considered that his looks betokened a man of strength and iron will. He was the sort of man who gained a great deal of satisfaction through the simple act of observing his reflection through a mirror each morning.

Dvan leaned back in his chair. It creaked a mild protest under the burden. Then looking at Duke he said: 'Are you *nombres huit cinq zero deux*?'

Duke answered quietly: '*Oui, mon officer*. That is my number.'

'Are you on the records under the name of Duke Connor, born a citizen of the United States, who swore allegiance to the *regiments étrangers* of France?'

Duke told him it was so.

Dvan licked his lips with a vivid red tongue and proceeded to put the same questions of identity to Cream and Biggin. He was enjoying this formality. It gave him a sensation of massive importance, which was altogether agreeable.

That done, Dvan intoned the charges, quoting the various regulations involved. Then, after drawing heavily on the cheroot that by now had turned the atmosphere into a single rolling cloud, he announced: 'I will hear your defence.'

Duke said: '*Mon officier*, my comrades have empowered me to speak for all of us . . .'

Then, speaking slowly and with care, he recounted each episode as he knew it until the point where they were arrested in the desert.

It took a long time and he was not interrupted once.

After the first minute Dvan forgot about his cheroot. He let it burn pungently between his stubby fingers. As he listened to the description of the working in the mountain valley his pig-like eyes seemed to become suffused with blood. They glared red and vicious.

When at last the story was complete Major Dvan turned sharply to Lieutenant Blum, who was standing slightly to the rear of his chair.

'*Mon Dieu!* This is exactly what they told you when you arrested them, is it not?'

Blum nodded eagerly.

'*Mais oui*. In substance it is the same.'

'Then either they are mad or they think we are mad! But the Legion articles of war do not make allowances for the mental condition of soldiers.'

Duke forbore to make the obvious retort.

Major Dvan slowly placed both elbows on his desk in what he imagined to be an impressive gesture of firm authority. His bloodshot eyes were glinting.

Once, many years before, he had been a spectator at a court martial of deserters. There he had heard the presiding officer make a scathing speech to the accused before condemning them to death. Ever since, Major Dvan had retained vivid memories of that speech. Whole extracts had remained in his mind. Often he had hoped for a chance to use them himself as though they were his own. Now that chance had arrived. In truth, everything came to he who waited . . .

'I find you each guilty of the foulest crime of which a soldier can be responsible,' he said. 'You refused the burden of arms, you deserted those who were your comrades . . . '

Major Dvan was warming up nicely. The words he had first heard so long ago were reproducing well. He was well satisfied with his performance.

' . . . but you did more than that. You denied and defied the solemn oath of allegiance that you freely gave on the day that you enlisted. You have shown yourselves not only to be men of no courage, but also to be men of no honour.

The Legion that you deserted no longer wants you. But it would be an insult to those thousands who so loyally serve the Tricolour if you did not pay the fullest penalty. My order is that you be shot twelve hours from now — which is nine tomorrow morning.'

14

Unused Bullets

Traditionally, those who are about to die are allowed facilities so that they may be better able to contemplate their fate. Some are provided with a good meal. Others are allowed to sleep on a soft and clean bed. It depends on the place and the circumstances. The Legion was no exception. The Legion articles of war laid it down that condemned men must not be fettered during their last few hours of life. Their hands must be free so that they may write last letters if they so wish — and if they are capable of writing. Their legs must be untrammelled so that they may exercise within the confines of their prison.

Thus, immediately they were returned to the guardroom Duke, Cream and Biggin had their irons taken off. An oil lamp was lit in the place and a supply of paper and pencils left on the bench.

But they did not make use of their strictly limited freedom. They did not even use the writing materials. They sat. That was all. Just sat, looking fixedly at nothing.

They must have been like that for two hours or more when Duke suddenly spoke. His voice had a rough, brittle edge.

He said: 'Sooner or later every fort in Morocco will have to be told that we're missing on a confidential mission. I figure it'll be sooner. The only reason Major Pylo hasn't done anything about it yet will be because of the need for secrecy. But we've been gone almost a week now. He must have got hold of the idea that things ain't exactly right with us.'

Cream grunted and rubbed his bandaged wound.

'If you're hopin' something's gonna happen before that firing squad takes over you're askin' too much. That sorta miracle just don't happen.'

'Maybe . . . but it'd give us just that extra chance if we could hold up the execution party for a while — even if it was just a short while.'

Cream and Biggin jerked their heads towards him. Biggin summarised what they were both thinking.

'Cor luv it,' he said. 'What do yer want us to do? Start a private war with our bare 'ands!'

'No, that wasn't exactly what I was gonna suggest. But have you figured what would happen if we could cause just an hour's delay? Maybe you haven't, so I'll tell you. That durned fool of a commandant would have to hold an enquiry. The enquiry would only be a formality and I guess it wouldn't take so long. But it might help. All in all we might put off the death party until the afternoon. Something *might* happen by then. I have a hunch Pylo will be getting out some kinda message mighty soon. He just can't delay much longer.'

Cream glanced out through the barred window then at the heavy steel door.

'Ah can't see any way outa here,' he said.

'I wasn't thinking of getting out. I was thinking of staying in — staying in here longer than they want us to.'

They didn't reply. They both looked at him with expressions of dazed astonishment.

Duke went on: 'That door opens inwards, like most jail doors. This is a mighty heavy bench we're sitting on. I figure we could fix that bench so the door won't open so easy. In fact, they may have to organise a battering ram to break in.' He paused then added almost fiercely. 'Sure, I know it sounds crazy. Maybe it is crazy. But ain't anything better than just sitting here like three scared rabbits waiting to be shot?'

Biggin rubbed his thin face.

'It'd just be putting it orf at the best,' he said.

Duke got to his feet and stood over him.

'As long as we put it off we have just that much more chance. Sure, I realise it won't take them so long to break in but if the execution doesn't take place at the set time there just has to be an enquiry and a new time fixed. That's military law and I've a hunch the Major here worships military law.'

They relapsed into another period of heavy silence. It was Cream who finally broke it. He stood up beside Duke and made a playful feint at him with his fist.

'Ah've always followed you up to now,' he said. 'Ah guess there ain't no reason why to stop.'

They both looked at Biggin. There was a taut grin on the Cockney's face.

'Blimey,' he told them. 'I never thought I'd get round to trying to keep myself *in* clink . . .'

Because they had no means of knowing the exact time, Duke decided it was best to fix the barricade immediately. There was a chance that a routine call might be made before the time came for the execution and the obstruction would be discovered. But that was a possibility that just had to be accepted.

The bench was rather over five feet long. It was constructed of heavy teak and no part of it was less than four inches thick. It had probably been there since the day, more than fifty years before, when Fort Ducane was built.

The lock on the steel door was fixed

some four feet above floor level and it protruded slightly both on the inside and out.

Moving silently, they carried the bench over to the door. There they upended it so that one end was on the ground and the other wedged beneath the lock. That done, the door could not be opened without either breaking the lock or the bench. Most likely the bench would break first, but a lot of pressure would be needed before it did so.

When they had finished Duke felt acutely aware of the puny manner in which they were trying to cheat death. Just a block of wood between them and a morning firing squad. But something within him said that the effort was worthwhile. He had the same fear of death as any normal man. But he had faced it many times before without flinching. He knew that it was not cowardice that had inspired the device. It was the natural will to live combined with something else . . . with a desire for justice, perhaps. Justice for himself and the two men who had shared so much with him.

For some reason that they could not understand, they smiled at each other as they lay on the stone floor and prepared to rest, but not to sleep.

★   ★   ★

They heard the steps outside. Many steps. They heard the grating sound as the lock turned. Then silence. Silence as pressure was used against a door, which refused to move.

Slowly they rose from the floor and stood against the wall. Each of them watched that door. Watched it almost fearfully and with an eternity of strain showing in their eyes.

From outside, a grey and unhealthy light was coming through the barred window.

They heard a mumble of voices. Puzzled and angry voices Then a single voice came through. There was no mistaking it. It was that of Major Dvan. Yet somehow it sounded different from the time they last heard it. The self-satisfied richness had gone from it. In comparison, it was almost thin and reedy.

163

'Are you men mad?' he asked. 'You must have jammed this door. Open it at once!'

Cream and Biggin looked at Duke. He shrugged his shoulders and turned away. There was no point in answering him. There was nothing to be said.

Then Duke noticed the light from the window again.

This was the light of the very early dawn. Of five o'clock, maybe. Certainly not much later. And their execution was not to take place until nine . . .

And this could not be some pre-execution routine visit, otherwise the commandant himself would not be there.

Duke felt his heart swell so that for a second he could scarcely breathe. Perhaps a message had arrived from Pylo at Dana Talani!

Major Dvan spoke again. This time it was almost in a shriek.

'Fools! You must come out at once. I wish to question you again. Five new deserters have arrived at the fort. They were lost in the sandstorm. They say you left them at the oasis and their story bears out your own . . . '

164

15

Vengeance of the Slaves

The change was almost more than Dvan could tolerate. He had been well satisfied with himself. He had congratulated himself on the prompt manner with which he had sentenced three deserters who had put up such a preposterous story as a defence. Then, while he was still abed, five other legionnaires dressed in Arab robes had been sighted from the fort. Although mounted on camels, they made no attempt at flight. They were lost, weary and thirsty. It seemed almost as though they were glad that they had by chance stumbled on Fort Ducane.

They had told a story which fitted in all of its details with that offered by the American legionnaire. It was fantastic, but nonetheless it was so.

He sat heavily in his desk chair and blinked at Duke. Then he transferred his attention to Cream and Biggin. He decided that he still did not like any of them. They had made him look a fool. Soon the entire garrison would know that he had wrongly condemned them and they had only been saved by a lucky chance. Or had he been wrong . . . Certainly he could take no action on their story until he received confirmation from Dana Talani. And since it had not been thought worthwhile to equip Fort Ducane with wireless, he might have to wait a long time.

With that fact resting heavily on his mind he lighted a cheroot, then said: 'It is possible that there is some truth in what you told me. Anyway, it will have to be investigated. I have decided in this instance to overlook the ridiculous action of barring yourselves in the guardroom. Therefore you will from now on share normal garrison duties in this fort. You will report to Lieutenant Blum. He will arrange for you to draw uniforms and equipment.'

Duke blinked at Dvan. He felt bewilderment blended with a sense of muffled fury.

'But *mon officier* . . . what about the mine? The first load of uranium may be leaving there at any time. It would be a disaster if it got into the wrong hands. With respect *mon officier*, can you not take some immediate action?'

Major Dvan raised a fat fist. He was going to crash it down, on his desk. Just in time he realised that it would not be either a dignified or impressive gesture. He lowered the fist gently.

'Action! *Ma foi*, but what sort of action can I take? If your story is true, then certainly a force must be sent to investigate. But more detailed information than you have given will be needed. You say yourself that without a guide it is impossible to find the valley. The first necessity will be to find someone who can guide a strong force through the mountains!'

Duke very nearly groaned aloud. Nearly, but not quite. In spite of his anxiety, in spite of his fatigue, he still retained the essentials of discipline. So he said as quietly as possible: 'That may be so, *mon officier*. But on the other hand

I'm sure we can find the rough locality where the track through the mountains begins. It is only twenty miles from the oasis, and that oasis ought not to be hard to find. If men can be spread across that area we may intercept the supplies as they are leaving the valley for the coast. The man Toole told me that they take that same route.'

Dvan looked regretfully out of the window. The sun was well up now and the heat was mounting. If all had gone according to plan these three malcontents would at this moment be facing the firing squad, instead of which they were having the insolence to stand there arguing with him just because someone in Dana Talani had been fool enough to give them a task of responsibility. He decided to put a stop to the nonsense. He cleared his throat. As he drew in a breath he noticed for the first time the figure in the doorway. It was leaning against the wall, legs crossed. Both hands were thrust deep into the front pockets of his breeches. There was an air of studied insolence about this man's dark face. He was in the sand-grimed uniform of a captain.

The captain smiled. It was a grim kind of smile. Then he said: '*Bonjour. mon officier*. I'm D'Avalon from Dana Talani. I've come under the orders of Major Pylo.'

Duke forgot that he was supposed to be standing to attention. Cream and Biggin forgot it too. They all wheeled round when they heard the familiar voice.

D'Avalon detached himself from the wall. He nodded to the legionnaires and strolled towards Dvan. The major struggled to make a show of welcome. But it was difficult. This captain seemed to take over control of affairs without saying anything and before he had been in the room more than a minute. Dvan could sense that he was no longer the dominant person in the fort, even though he was the commandant. He would never be the dominant person so long as this tense-looking and restless officer was about.

Dvan said: 'I'm glad you have arrived, *mon capitaine*, and I think I know the reason for it. These legionnaires claim they have been acting as agents and . . . '

D'Avalon interrupted. And he did not interrupt politely. There was something almost insolent about the way he cut in. But Dvan found that he was not inclined to engage in a verbal tussle. Perhaps he did not dare to do so.

D'Avalon said: 'That is quite true. They have been agents on a most dangerous undertaking. When I arrived here a few minutes ago to pass information about them I met Lieutenant Blum. He told me of the experiences they have endured. Of course, the information they have gained is vital and what the legionnaire has just been saying is correct. We must attempt to prevent the uranium leaving the mountains. For that purpose we'll need as many men as you can spare — perhaps more than you can spare.'

Dvan wanted to refuse. He wanted to point out that he alone was commandant of the fort and that he would not have the garrison weakened. He wanted to put this officer in his place . . .

But instead he nodded.

'It is as you wish, *capitaine*,' he said.

Two companies were detached from

the fort for the march to the Atlas Mountains. This, with the men that D'Avalon had brought with him from Dana Talani, made a total of three hundred.

They left within two hours of D'Avalon's arrival at the fort and, because speed was the first essential, they had discarded the more usual marching order. They left in battle order — no packs on their backs, nothing to carry except arms, ammunition, water, and hard rations.

Duke, Cream and Biggin, having been re-equipped at the fort, were deliberately placed in the front file directly behind D'Avalon and Sergeant Collat. It was Sergeant Collat who, having heard their description of the oasis, was almost certain he could identify it.

'It's too small to be marked on the maps,' he told D'Avalon. 'I don't think it even has a name. But I called there once with a patrol. It is as the legionnaires say, about twenty miles from the Atlas foothills and I'm almost certain I can lead you to it.'

That was a big stroke of luck, Collat had had almost a lifetime's experience in the desert and he would not make such a claim lightly.

That march was hell. The concentrated essence of hell. It lasted for two days with only five hours' sleep during the nights. Other rest periods were cut to the absolute minimum. In the daytime the cruel sun grilled them. In the night the chill winds froze them. And all the time the soft, unrelenting sand pulled at their boots, blew into their eyes and mouths.

But Sergeant Collat was right. He did know the oasis. And guided them directly to it.

Duke recognised it when they were still half a mile off. And as they drew close there was a hollow flapping, which developed in intensity until it reached a crescendo, which filled the air. Then scores of vultures rose like a blanket and circled angrily above them. But already there was little left of the three men who had been left there. Only torn clothes through which there peeped white bones.

D'Avalon ordered that each man replenish his water bottle. This was done, but there was still no rest. Within thirty minutes of arriving they marched away from the shade of the oasis and still on towards the Atlas foothills.

During the last two days D'Avalon had spent much time in questioning Duke on the details of the valley. He did this with the meticulous care of a trained soldier who will leave as little as possible to chance before committing his men to action. He even got Duke to draw a rough sketch map of the valley for him, with the machine gun emplacements marked.

This puzzled Duke, because he could not see much prospect of their finding their way to the valley. He mentioned it to D'Avalon. The captain agreed.

'I fear you are right,' he said. 'The valley may never be found and it may be that all we'll ever be able to do will be to make it useless by sealing it off. That, however, would be a terribly wasteful operation. It would require the perma-nent stationing of hundreds of men at the foothills and perhaps even the building of a new fort. I think that in the end the general staff will insist that at least some attempt is made to find it.'

'I figure that won't be necessary,' Duke told him. 'The supplies in that place won't last forever. If it's sealed off properly the folks inside it will have to come out eventually, unless they want to die of starvation. Then we may be able to persuade some of them to show us the route.'

It was Collat who interrupted them. As usual, the N.C.O.'s sharp eyes had been searching the desert. They suddenly fixed on a spot that was at a thirty degrees bearing due south. A very distant spot. Immediately he trotted up to D'Avalon and said: '*Mon officier* . . . many men are moving towards the mountains.'

The order to halt was given and the long column shuffled to a grateful stop. For hours past they had been moving as though in a nightmare, their backs bent, their heads drooping forward with fatigue. Any pause, however brief, was accepted thankfully.

D'Avalon pulled out his field glasses and trained them on the spot to which Collat was pointing. He watched for only a few seconds. Then he passed the glasses to Duke.

'*Mon legionnaire* . . . is that not a peculiar sight?' he asked.

Duke adjusted the focus. Then what he saw forced him to take in a deep breath. He saw Arabs. Maybe a hundred of them. Men, women and even children. Most were riding mules and a few were on camels. They were moving towards the foothills. And they were being escorted by several men in European dress. Men who were mounted on horses. The course they were taking would bring them across the position on which the legionnaire column was standing and also very close to it.

Duke mentioned this to D'Avalon when he handed back the glasses.

'It's almost certainly another bunch of slaves moving in,' he said. 'That European escort makes it a cinch. They'll be the entire population of some village. I figure they'll pass mighty close to this spot and they haven't seen us yet.'

'I know,' D'Avalon said. 'At the moment they are only just visible to us, and that's because they are mounted. We are on foot and cannot be seen so easily by them . . . I think we will wait for these

175

people, *mon legionnaire*. And I think also we will make it a surprise. I do not want them to be able to run off. *Mon sergent*, the column will lie flat and make no noise.'

Collat gave the order and the line of legionnaires fell to their bellies, facing in the direction of the approaching Arabs.

Kneeling, D'Avalon watched again through his glasses, Then he once more spoke to the sergeant.

'If I give the order to fire it must only be at the European escort,' he said. 'Great care must be taken to see none of the Arabs is hurt. Particularly the women and children. In any case, the first rounds must be fired only at the Europeans' horses so as to dismount them. They will only be fired at directly if they persist in trying to escape.

'*Je comprend, mon capitaine.*'

Collat crawled away to deliver the order along the line.

It was a long wait and it was an uneasy wait. Even the weary men in the column seemed to be aware of the tension as they pressed close to the sand and fingered the breech bolts of their Lebels.

Duke shared with them all the nerve twisting anxiety of at first not being able to see the Arabs. For long minutes of utter silence he wondered whether in fact they were there at all. Perhaps they had changed direction and were already lost to their sight while the column crouched stupidly here. Many wild fears went through his mind.

Then they heard them.

It was almost uncanny to hear them long before being able to see them. Like preparing to come to grips with a ghost.

Faintly at first, then louder, they heard the crunch of hooves pressing into the sand. Then the creaking and clinking if bridles. A snatch of Arabic talk. A burst of laughter. The bawling of some child . . . Wretches going willingly to an unsuspected hell.

Duke glanced anxiously at D'Avalon. A lot depended on the right timing from him. If he attempted to intercept them too soon they might break away. On the other hand, the same might happen if he waited too long. Much depended on

Captain D'Avalon.

D'Avalon himself showed no traces of nerves. Whatever he may have felt, he never showed emotion in times of emergency. It was at such times that his mind seemed to go on ice. He had dedicated his life to military science. A fundamental part of that science was to be able to do the right thing at precisely the right time. It probably never occurred to him that he would fail.

And he didn't fail on this occasion.

The heads of the Arabs became visible. By a stroke of fortune, they were advancing directly on the column and not slightly past it, as had been expected.

The order had been given to the legionnaires that they were to watch D'Avalon and rise when he did. D'Avalon waited until the moment when they were actually spotted by some of the Arabs. It was then that he sprang to his feet — at the second when they began their excited gesticulating and had reined their mounts.

The column followed him instantly. It was as though they had suddenly emerged from out of the sand. A startled cry went up from the Arabs and some of the mules reared to their hind legs. Then they looked with baffled astonishment at the line of armed men that barred their path.

It was now possible to see that four Europeans were with the Arabs. Duke recognised one of them. It was Flavoni, the Italian.

D'Avalon spoke to the Europeans. He did so in French and he did not waste words.

'I wish to speak with you, *messieurs*. Get off your horses and walk towards me. If there is any attempt to escape you will be shot.'

Flavoni was apparently their leader, for the three others looked towards him. The fat Italian gazed wildly at D'Avalon. He attempted a bluff.

'What do you mean by barring our way in this manner? The desert is free to all, is it not? By what right do you do this to . . . '

His words died away. He saw Duke. Then he saw Cream and Biggin. His swarthy face was suddenly loose and flabby. For the moment he seemed incapable of speaking further. D'Avalon took over for him.

'*Messieurs* . . . I see you recognise your old companions.'

Flavoni still gaped helplessly. This was more than he could readily absorb. His mental processes were numbed by shock.

When D'Avalon spoke again there was a change in his voice. It cut through the fetid air like the lash of a long whip.

'I told you to come here! Do as I say — unless you want to die! That applies to your companions, also.'

Slowly the Europeans dismounted. Equally slowly, they walked towards D'Avalon. Behind them the Arabs watched, scarcely understanding.

They halted in front of D'Avalon. Duke said to the lieutenant: 'This Italian was in the valley when we were there. He didn't say much then, but he looked like he had plenty of influence around the place.'

D'Avalon nodded. Then to Flavoni he said: 'You will appreciate that the product of the valley is a secret no longer. I now intend that instead of taking these wretched Arabs there, you will take us.'

'Take you to the valley? But no! Nothing would make me do that . . . I do not know the way . . . other guides were to take us there.'

Flavoni's eyes widened. He hitched his breeches over his bowed legs in a gesture of contempt.

With almost casual precision D'Avalon un-strapped the cover of his revolver holster. Then he pulled out the weapon. He levelled it at a point between Flavoni's eyes.

'I hope you are not serious, *monsieur*. It will be a pity to see a stubborn man die, but die you must if you refuse my request. Are you ready to die, *monsieur*?'

Flavoni looked into the black void of the revolver. His jaw was unhinged.

'*Si*! I will show you . . . But what of me? Will you then allow me to go free in return?'

D'Avalon ignored the question. He put one of his own.

'How long will it take my column to reach the valley?'

One of the other Europeans who had

so far recovered as to want to ingratiate himself gave the answer.

'On foot, it will be daylight tomorrow if you rest during the night.'

Half to himself, D'Avalon said: 'This time I think the men will have a full night's rest, even if it must be in the Atlas Mountains. I fear they will have much to do tomorrow.'

Then to Flavoni he said: 'Where do these Arabs come from?'

'From the village of Rapal.'

'Then tell them they must return to Rapal. And say that all others who are working in the valley will soon be back in their villages.'

★　★　★

They slept for seven hours that night on one of the tracks in the mountains. Or probably it would be more accurate to say that they rested. Without blankets and in the comparative cold, few of the legionnaires actually slept.

And all the time ten men were detailed to keep guard on the four Europeans.

It would have been a lot quicker if a very few legionnaires had made use of the available horses and camels which grazed in the foothills, but D'Avalon decided against this course. He resolved only to arrive at the valley in strength. Therefore the whole column moved laboriously on foot. Even D'Avalon refused to consider riding and, to their disgust, the Europeans had their horses taken from them.

The only incident on the journey was when a handful of hapless Arab guards emerged to challenge them. They blinked uncomprehendingly when they saw the great column of legionnaires. They then dropped their carbines and threw up their hands . . .

A few minutes before they were due to emerge from the pass on to the side of the valley D'Avalon made yet another close study of the map Duke had drawn.

He murmured: 'It's those machine guns that worry me. They must be seized very quickly, yet I'm not sure how it can be done without great casualties.'

Duke heard the muttered words. He could not help. Those gun posts were cunningly located and they had a clear field of fire. There was no cover on the approaches to any of them.

The sun was at its zenith when they emerged on to the lip of the valley. There was not a single legionnaire among the hundreds there who did not look with astonishment at the spectacle that was spread before him.

Even Duke, who had seen it all before, was fascinated by that vista of green vegetation, of dotted dwellings.

It looked almost idyllic. A scene of peace. And because of that, the evil and the misery that were in truth concealed down there seemed to be worse.

As he assessed the situation Captain D'Avalon turned to Duke.

'Your map was very accurate, legionnaire,' he said.

Then D'Avalon started to group his men. They were divided into three sections. One section, under Sergeant Collat, circled the top of the valley so as to reach the distant side and place themselves directly over the entrance to the mine. Another section, commanded

184

by a corporal, was detailed to descend into the valley but to remain at that end of it where they would be out of range of the clearly visible machine gun posts. The third section, under D'Avalon himself, with Duke, Cream and Biggin, were to advance towards the mine through the valley in the hope that there would be no resistance. If, however, resistance did come, the first section was to seize the mine entrance while the other under the corporal tackled the machine guns. The disposition of D'Avalon's own men would depend on a decision on the spot. They would, in fact, be a tactical reserve.

There was no attempt on the part of the men to conceal themselves. There was no reason to do so. They moved openly into their positions.

And as they did so, the Arabs who had been toiling in and out of the mine entrance seemed to stop in their work and stare upwards to the top of the valley. At that distance, though, it was doubtful whether they'd be able to recognise the arrivals as legionnaires. That would come later, when Collat's section got nearer the mine.

Then Arabs started to emerge from their stone dwellings and they joined those at the mine. Within minutes, hundreds of them had gathered and all were looking up towards the legionnaires. Duke thought they had the appearance of a hive of brown ants.

Before they moved into the valley D'Avalon gave a final order to his men.

'We are not here to fight unless we have to,' he said. 'If there is fighting, then helpless people will be killed. I do not want that to happen. But nonetheless, we will be prepared. *Legionnaires . . . bayonettes!*'

There was a shuffle along the line of one hundred men, then an almost simultaneous click from their rifles as the bayonets were clipped under the barrels. They moved into the valley and towards the mine entrance, a winding column of men, their rifles held ready.

They had reached the bottom of the valley when they noticed the three machine guns. Each was trained on them. Duke felt his scalp turn hot, as though acid had been poured on it.

They marched past the now empty dwellings. They drew level with the huts.

It was there that Toole was waiting. He was standing at the entrance to the big hut, just as he had been when Duke had first arrived with Cream and Biggin. Except that Flavoni was no longer with him. Flavoni was under guard at the rear of the column with his three friends. But Toole was not alone. A dozen or more men stood with him.

Clever-looking men. No doubt they were chemists, as Toole had said. But men without scruples, without the capacity for pity.

D'Avalon halted his section. The men lowered their rifle butts to the ground. Then he moved alone towards Toole.

Toole was watching him closely, his lips twisted in a caricature of a smile

D'Avalon began: '*Monsieur*, I understand . . . '

The machine guns opened fire.

All three of them were trained on the one section, on the hundred men. If those guns had been in the hands of trained soldiers, not one legionnaire could possibly have lived. As it was, a score of them were killed or wounded in the first few seconds. Then D'Avalon gave his order.

His shrill, penetrating voice rose above the clatter of the guns.

'Seize the huts!'

It was the obvious move. Those huts gave some form of cover against the bullets. The legionnaires gathered themselves for the rush.

But they didn't make it. They did not even have time in which to start the first step. They were caught by a new attack. An attack from the Arabs.

They swept into and through the line of legionnaires like a wild sea. Some were holding picks and axes and shovels from the mine as weapons. Others had seized stones and sticks. They streamed into the huts, they swept up the sides of the valley to the gun posts. The women were there with their men. Their screams of fury seemed to tear the air. This was their vengeance. This was the vengeance of the Arab slaves.

Few of those who attacked the guns

were killed or even wounded. Before this sudden unleashing of the horde the gunners lost their nerve and tried to flee.

But there was nowhere for them to flee to. They were trapped in their own prison. They were to be the victims of their own prisoners.

For a brief moment Duke caught a glimpse of Toole. He was pressed against the wall of the shed. Hundreds of Arabs were screaming and pressing around him. Toole's face was contorted into a hideous mask of fear. Then the mob fell on him . . .

At the same moment the valley trembled as a massive explosion came from the mine entrance. Duke knew what that sound meant. Some of the Arabs had exploded those cases of T.N.T.

★　★　★

It is no contradiction in terms to say that things can change yet remain the same.

Take that valley in the Atlas Mountains, for example.

The mine there is still being worked.

189

Arabs are still labouring in it. But the place is no longer a hell of suffering. It is equipped properly now and those who work in it are properly protected and free to leave at any time they wish.

Legionnaires are still there, too. But they are not deserters. They are units of the Morocco Command whose task it is to guard the security of the valley with its precious mineral.

There are, however, three legionnaires who will never serve in that valley. In fact they will never be ordered to go anywhere near the Atlas Mountains again. That undertaking was given to them by Major Pylo at their own request. There was one other request he granted Legionnaires Duke, Cream and Biggin. He said he'd see that they never at any time had to serve under Major Dvan.

THE END

Other titles in the
Linford Mystery Library:

DENE OF THE SECRET SERVICE

Gerald Verner

Bound for Liverpool to board his Japanese ship, *Oki Maru*, a Korean seaman is murdered and his identity assumed by his killer. Then, after the ship sails, it disappears — presumed lost in a storm . . . The owner of a remote country house in Wales is pressured into selling it — then brutally murdered. Meanwhile, when secret documents relating to a draft treaty with Japan go missing from the Foreign Office, agent Dene of the Secret Service has orders to recover them . . .

LONELY ROAD MURDER

John Russell Fearn

Rosemary Lennox is horrified to find her best friend and neighbour, Mary Francis, strangled in her flat and it's not long before her husband, John Francis, is also murdered there too. The police question Rosemary, her friend and fellow lodger Bob McDonnell and their landlady Ellen Moreland, but they are unable to establish a motive. However, when Rosemary and Bob attempt to investigate, she discovers that all the evidence points to her friend . . .

THE HAUNTED GALLERY

John Russell Fearn

Baffling robberies and mysterious murders are the stock-in-trade of Miss Victoria Lincoln, private detective . . . After Professor Marchant dies, his house, Bartley Towers, is visited nightly by a sinister enemy, which frequents the gallery containing the Professor's collection of antiques and curios. When the detective investigates the case, she calls on the assistance of Caroline Gerrard . . . Thereafter, Miss Lincoln and Miss Gerrard investigate a series of bizarre cases, which are seemingly insoluble . . . until Victoria Lincoln gets to work . . .